NOTHING SACRED

NOTHING SACRED

LORI HAHNEL

*To Dolly:
Thanks so much for the support! All the best,
Lori*

thistledown press

©Lori Hahnel, 2009
All rights reserved

No part of this publication may be reproduced or transmitted in any form or by any means, graphic, electronic or mechanical, including photocopying, recording, or any information storage and retrieval system, without permission in writing from the publisher or a licence from The Canadian Copyright Licensing Agency (Access Copyright). For an Access Copyright licence, visit www.accesscopyright.ca or call toll free to 1-800-893-5777.

Thistledown Press Ltd.
633 Main Street
Saskatoon, Saskatchewan, S7H 0J8
www.thistledownpress.com

Library and Archives Canada Cataloguing in Publication
Hahnel, Lori
Nothing sacred / Lori Hahnel.
ISBN 978-1-897235-63-8
I. Title.
PS8615.A365N68 2009   C813'.6   C2009-904213-4

Cover photograph: Hulton Archive/Getty Images
Cover and book design: Jackie Forrie
Printed and bound in Canada

Mixed Sources
Cert no. SW-COC-001271
© 1996 FSC
FSC

Thistledown Press gratefully acknowledges the financial assistance of the Canada Council for the Arts, the Saskatchewan Arts Board, and the Government of Canada through the Book Publishing Industry Development Program for its publishing program.

Canada Council for the Arts   Conseil des Arts du Canada   SASKATCHEWAN ARTS BOARD   Canadian Heritage   Patrimoine canadien

To my mother and my father

Contents

9	Leading Men
19	Nothing Sacred
27	Art is Long
37	We Had Faces Then
48	Blue Lake
56	Rain in December
65	The Least She Could Do
72	You Ain't Goin' Nowhere
85	The Pass
91	Across the Universe
103	Hamburg Blues

108	You Tore Me Down
114	The Poor Little Rich Girl
126	The Selfish Professor
131	Sisters of Mercy
139	Beware of God
147	Bells and Whistles
157	Ghost Rag
166	Close to the Bone
174	Valediction
188	Fiction Romance

Leading Men

THE AFTERNOON MAUREEN AND I WENT TO see *A Day at the Races* it rained so hard that we heard it beat down on the roof during the movie. Down in the fourth row the rain even dripped in through the ceiling. The girl who sold us the cheesy-tasting popcorn they always had at The Plaza (was the butter old?) said she was moving back to Edinburgh, because it didn't rain as much there as it did here. Calgary's a dry place, but some years it pours all summer.

Usually I'd take smoke breaks during the musical numbers in Marx Brothers movies, but this time something made me stay. Harpo played Strauss, for one thing, which I always enjoy. Then I noticed the intent look on his face. And his sinewy forearms plucking the harp's strings. His nose, his lips, his curly hair. Okay, wig.

"Hey," I whispered to Maureen. "Don't you think he looks like David?"

"David Liebkind?"

"Yeah."

"I guess so."

NOTHING SACRED

Maureen never liked my old boyfriend David much. Can't say I really did anymore, either. Musicians, eh?

As I listened to "On the Beautiful Blue Danube" it struck me that all my serious romantic interests resembled Harpo Marx in one way or another. David had his general build, his sinewy arms, a similar nose and curly hair (though black and not a wig) and played clarinet, not the harp. Still. Sean had looked a bit like Harpo, though *his* hair was red and he'd been pretty quiet. He wasn't around long enough to tell what he might have said given the chance. Luke had been the most Harpoesque of all. Actually, with his glasses on, he'd reminded me of a tall, blond Woody Allen, if you can picture that. When he took his glasses off, he was a ringer for Harpo. He could even pull a Gookie, that weird expression Harpo modeled after a cigar roller in his Lower East Side neighbourhood. And then Luke was trying to break into standup, last I heard. So all of my boyfriends reminded me of Harpo in some way, except for Kirk.

Kirk was unlike anyone I'd ever been interested in before. He looked a little like a blond Paul McCartney, kind of a dirty-blond hiker Paul McCartney. His blue eyes were flecked with yellow, his teeth glowed against his tanned skin. I have to say, Kirk didn't remind me of Harpo at all.

༄

"John Derek," said James, as he poured me another glass of wine. "There's a hot movie star for you, Liz. John Derek in *The Ten Commandments*. Yum."

"Ugh, no. He's so tanned he looks like he's made of caramel. And he's too short."

Leading Men

It rained again the night my neighbour James and I made dinner at his place for Kirk. I made a shrimp risotto and James made the appetizer (figs and Parmigiano-Reggiano, thinly sliced) and dessert (fresh strawberries with balsamic vinegar). He and Maureen both worked at the Safeway on Eighth Street, so we got a deal on all the food. By ten the risotto was cold and there was still no sign of Kirk. James and I had polished the figs and cheese and though neither of us said anything, we were becoming annoyed.

James had started to drink mid-afternoon and was now quite flushed, and that high-lift blond he used made his face look deep pink. I have to admit, when Maureen first brought him around, I didn't care much for him. He was always partying as far as I could see. And he was one of these people that knew something about everything or knew someone who'd done it. I didn't have much patience with that, but I was slowly warming up to him. We both liked to cook, and anybody who loved movies as much as he did couldn't be all bad.

"All right," he said. "Randolph Scott."

"Yeah, he's okay. A little too rugged for me, though. Now, Leslie Howard, he's one of my favourites."

James shook his head. "No, no. He's too — I don't know — pasty. Just doesn't do it for me at all. How about Peter O'Toole?"

"I always think of Groucho's remark that he has a double-phallic name. What about Errol Flynn?"

"He's pretty good."

"Errol Flynn in *Captain Blood*, before he ruined his liver and got all puffy and bloated. He was hot."

"Mmm, not hot. He was nice-looking, not hot."

"He was hot," I insisted. "Okay, Spencer Tracy."

"Spencer Tracy? Why not Harpo Marx? Spencer Tracy gets your vote for the title of Hottest Movie Star Ever?"

"Well, maybe not *ever*. But don't underestimate the charm of the Irish."

"You're insane. What about James Dean?"

"James Dean was okay. But he was too short."

James and I could go on like that for hours. In fact we did go on like that until past midnight. We ate the most of the risotto and the strawberries. There was no answer at Kirk's place. We drank a lot of wine and never did agree on the Hottest Movie Star Ever. We seemed to have pretty different taste when it came to men.

So how did we both end up being attracted to Kirk?

∞

Kirk was a surveyor for a seismic company. He was the guy who held the stick while another guy looked through the leveling instrument. Sounded boring as hell to me, but he didn't mind it. He thought my job, working in a bookstore, was the most boring thing he could think of. Surveying paid well and he could pick and choose when he worked. The only problem was — for me, not for him — that he'd be away for weeks at a time. He'd work for a few months in camps in northern Alberta or BC and spend the winter traveling. He'd been all over Western Europe and Central America, and planned to spend the coming winter in Japan and Thailand.

We met when he came into the store looking for the latest *Lonely Planet* guide for Thailand. We had a hard time keeping

Leading Men

Lonely Planet guides in the store, anyway, but those hikers cleaned us out of all the books on Thailand. We started to talk about how he travelled and how I would like to travel, and the next day he was back in the store wondering if I wanted to go for coffee.

∽

James and Kirk and I spent a lot of nights that summer in my kitchen smoking the black hash that James seemed to have a never-ending supply of. James always had contacts: no matter what you needed, he knew where to get it, or where to get the best deal. He was friends with the woman who owned both his house and the one next door, so when a suite on the main floor in the sister building opened up Maureen and I moved in. I loved it, although it had definitely seen better days. Haven't we all, as James said. It was built in 1912, like so many downtown houses — Calgary's first boom was in 1912 — and had hardwood floors and great six-inch baseboards, though they'd been painted over thousands of times. We had the main floor. Technically speaking, it was only a one-bedroom suite, but Maureen slept in what was the living room. Pocket doors separated her room from the living room, which was once the dining room. I slept in the bedroom, a little room off the kitchen, probably a pantry at one time.

Maureen would join us for a drink if she wasn't out with her boyfriend, but she wasn't a big smoker, so she'd usually head for bed earlier than us. Neither James nor I had to work until one, but she was on day shift. And Kirk, when he was in town, didn't have to worry about getting up at all.

Maybe I was wrong about this, but sometimes it seemed like it was a contest between James and me to see who could outlast the other, to see who'd fall asleep first, and the victor would get to spend time alone with Kirk. I thought for a while I had a little bit of an advantage because my bedroom was a few feet from the kitchen table where we sat. Then again, sometimes I just had to go to bed before they were ready to, and they'd move the party over to James's.

∽

The night they showed *Duck Soup* at The Plaza, I went with Kirk. He'd never seen a Marx Brothers movie before. Can you imagine? I mean, I'd never travelled, true. But he'd never seen a Marx Brothers movie. And I've noticed people's reactions to them are usually pretty polarized. Sometimes it's a gender thing. I know some women who love them, but a lot of women can't stand them. I was afraid Kirk wouldn't like the movie. And if he didn't like *Duck Soup*, their masterpiece, there was no hope. I had misgivings, frankly, but figured we'd have to give it a shot, see how our relationship weathered this litmus test.

Twenty minutes into it, he fell asleep. I woke him up and in a few minutes he fell asleep again. After waking him three times I gave up.

"Is it over already?" he asked when the house lights came up. The usher sweeping the front rows was the only other person in the theatre.

"You slept through most of it." I got up and made my way down the aisle.

Leading Men

He followed me. "Liz. I'm sorry. James and I were up late last night. I didn't get much sleep."

I couldn't think what to say to that, just walked out of the theatre, out onto Kensington Road. I wanted to ask him what he was doing over at James's, but I knew he only hung out with James because he was a dope slut. James was no fool, I'm sure he knew that. But Kirk was attractive, always had good stories about his trips. He looked at you like you were the only thing he was ever interested in. Even so, he was unreliable, impossible to pin down. I started to wonder if he wasn't using me just like he was using James.

Worse, how could I even be interested in a man who could sleep through *Duck Soup*?

༄

One afternoon off, I sat in the living room and read *While Rome Burns*, a collection of essays by Alexander Woollcott. It was kind of dry and I didn't get a lot of the references in it. My mind wandered to things like The Marx Brothers playing the Grand Theatre in Calgary when they were on the vaudeville circuit. It was the fourth largest theatre in Canada after it was built in 1912, so many big acts of the day played there: Sarah Bernhardt, Burns and Allen, Ethel Barrymore, Fred and Adele Astaire. And I used to work at the Grand. How weird is that? Anyway, Woollcott was a drama critic for *The New Yorker*, a member of the Algonquin Round Table in the twenties and thirties, as was Harpo Marx by virtue of their friendship. It had been rumoured that Woollcott was in love with Harpo. I was reading his book to see if I could gain any insight into that. I don't know why. Just the movie hound in me, I guess.

I was trying to decide whether I was really curious enough to keep slogging through it when Kirk called.

"Hey, great news. Change of plans. I'm going to Thailand next week."

"Next week? I thought you were going to work again for a couple of months before you left."

"Yeah, I was. But James has this travel agent friend who scored me a wicked deal on the flight, but only if I could leave next week, so I had to go for it. Isn't that cool?"

"Sure, I guess. It's kind of soon, though."

"Don't worry. You'll see lots of me before I go."

"What about tonight?"

"Yeah, I don't know. I have to go downtown and deal with my passport this afternoon, get my vaccinations, pick up some stuff. Can I call you later tonight?"

"Okay."

I knew he wouldn't call back that night. I didn't see him until three days later. I told James the news and James kept asking me if I'd seen him. When I finally did, he didn't call or anything, just showed up at the door at eleven o'clock.

"Hey, Liz. Glad you're still up."

"I was reading."

"*While Rome Burns*. What is that, a travel book?"

"No. It's a collection of essays."

"Essays. Crazy."

Later, tangled in his legs in bed, listening to the traffic, I thought about all the things I'd planned to say to him. What made him think he could just pick up and leave like that? What about the plans we'd made, the trip we were going to take to the U.K. in the spring? Or some spring, when I had the

Leading Men

money. All of a sudden we weren't talking about any of that anymore. But then I realized it didn't matter. This beautiful man asleep in my arms, this was the man who slept through *Duck Soup*. This was the man who stood James and me up for dinner without even giving us a good excuse. This was the man who said, "Essays. Crazy." This beautiful man would soon not be here anymore. And it didn't matter.

∽

Kirk's flight was at ten o'clock on Friday night. James had the windshield wipers on full speed on his Chevy Impala and we could still barely see anything except grey and lights. We could only see the headlights of the other cars on Barlow Trail on the way up to the airport, and the puddles at intersections swelled into lakes.

We'd planned to get Kirk up there in plenty of time to go through customs and all that, so we'd have time for a farewell drink. But of course he was late and we barely made it in time for his flight. Our goodbye was rushed, not as I pictured it (my version had better lighting and music by Max Steiner), but the reality was probably easier in the end.

He crushed me up against him and kissed me.

"Goodbye, kid. Keep reading all those crazy books, eh?"

"I will. Will you write me?"

"Of course."

I knew he wouldn't. He gave James a hug, waved at us and then he was gone.

"Let's order Manhattans," James said when we sat down in the airport lounge.

"God, no. At the airport? It'll cost a fortune."

"Look, I'm buying. It doesn't matter what you order here, it's all expensive. So you might as well get a good drink. And tonight we need a good drink."

"All right. You talked me into it."

After a couple of sips the Manhattan started to work on me. "You loved him, didn't you?" I asked.

James sighed. "Love is too strong a word. I liked him a whole lot. I lusted after him. But you loved him, I think."

"I don't know. I think I wanted to love him. I would have loved him."

"If he hadn't been such a jerk?"

"Well. If he'd been different, put it that way."

For a long time we didn't say anything, just watched the planes and the reflections of the lights on the wet runways outside. James chased the maraschino cherry in the bottom of his glass with the little plastic sword. After a while he spoke.

"Do you want to go to the midnight show at The Plaza?"

"What's showing?"

"I don't know. They're doing an Elizabeth Taylor fest. It might be *Suddenly Last Summer*."

"Oh, I'll see anything with Montgomery Clift in it. And anything by Tennessee Williams."

"And it's about cannibalism. It's the perfect movie."

"Exactly."

All the way to The Plaza, I thought this, though I wasn't going to say it. It was too much of a cliché. But I think we were both thinking it: this looked like the beginning of a beautiful friendship.

Nothing Sacred

THINGS ARE PRETTY QUIET UPSTAIRS; TRAVIS AND Noella aren't in their bedrooms. "Travis, Noely," I call into the closets. "Come out now." No giggles or whispers. I do a second round of the closets, in case they're huddled in the back. "This isn't funny. Come out now." Then I notice the front door is unlocked. I never leave the doors unlocked. Their jackets and boots are not on the bench by the door.

I look out the front window, then the back. "Travis!" I yell out the back door. "Noely!" I yell out the front, my voice suddenly sounding thin and reedy. My words disappear into the snow. Any footprints there might have been are covered now.

∼

I tried a new hairstyle a few mornings ago. Nobody noticed, but it's exactly the way Carole Lombard wore it in *My Man Godfrey*, bangs parted in the middle, probably to hide the scar on her forehead from the car accident. What must it have been like to work on that film with William Powell, her ex-husband?

It's just a good thing she didn't live to see that awful remake with that awful June Allyson. Can you imagine?

"See you at lunchtime, Travis," I called as he lined up to go in with the other first graders. I've often thought about the irony of Travis being called Travis. I'm sure his parents didn't call him after Travis Banton, I'm sure they have no idea who Travis Banton was. Maybe he's named after Travis Tritt, though I don't think they're much into country music. Maybe it's a family name, I don't know. Anyway, it's just funny that Travis Banton was one of Lombard's favourite costume designers. What are the chances?

I let Noely play at the playground a while, then she wanted to go. "Take me to the store, Ginny."

"We can't go to the store every time we drop Travis off at school. Let's go home and watch Rolie Polie Olie."

She shook her head, blond curls flying. "No. I wanna go to the store. Travis gets to go to school."

So we got into my car and drove over to the store. I was a little ashamed, a little worried that a neighborhood mom, or another nanny, might see us at Mac's at ten after nine every morning, as Noely filled her chubby fists with candy. I used to be better at this; I used to care more. Now, I figure a dollar's worth of candy buys me forty minutes of quiet. It's not like I'm abusing her, ignoring her. I just don't want to try to reason with a three year old. It can't be done. I tried with Travis and it was an exercise in futility. But I tried, dammit, I worked my ass off at it, and then I realized his parents let him do whatever he wanted at night and on weekends. So in spite of all my work, he's turning out to be a little shit, anyway. It makes me sad. I feel sorry for him, too. Now I think there's no point in trying to take the high road with Noely. If she wants candy from me, she gets it, no argument.

Two years ago the Martins said they wanted someone who'd be around until Noely started Grade One. I figured I could do that and they pay me well. Brad's a plastic surgeon and Shelley's an advertising executive, says she could never leave her job. Maybe she couldn't. But maybe kids need parents for more than a few hours between overtime and daybreak. Of course, I'd never say anything. I need this job.

Noely and I went home and read a few books and then she wanted to watch Olie in her room, so I had a few minutes to check out my new magazine. I took the bubble envelope out of my pack, slid the magazine in its plastic sleeve gently out. It's a January 1940 *Photoplay* I picked up on eBay for $10. It has that great old-magazine smell, brittle yellow pages. The article about Dorothy Lamour is missing, but Lombard's on the cover in a red and ivory silk brocade skirt and sleeveless blouse that bares her midriff, quite daring for the time. Her hair is dark blonde, shoulder length, off the face. The glossy red of her lipstick is the exact crimson of her garments. Lombard once said she'd made it in a man's world, but knew part of a woman's job was choosing the right shade of lipstick.

∞

When Mom had the stroke, I quit my job at the video store to look after her. Don't get the wrong idea, I'm not Florence Nightingale. I didn't want to do it, but there wasn't anyone else. My brother Jeff was in Toronto and Dad we hadn't heard from in years. I still lived at home, so that was that. The video store staff let me come in and borrow whatever I wanted, no charge, but most nights I was too damn tired to watch more than one.

When she got a spot in the home, it wasn't so bad. Then I thought I should go back to work at least part-time but she died soon after. Brad was a friend of Jeff's from high school and called to say they needed a nanny. They offered me twice what the video store paid and only occasional evenings or weekends. The thing was, we'd racked up some debt while Mom was sick. I couldn't have said no to the money if I'd wanted to.

∽

Travis and Noely are less interested in the playground after school now that the weather's cooling off. It's too bad, because if they don't work off some of that steam, they get owly by the time Shelley gets home. Maybe if they dressed more warmly, but they refuse to put on their winter jackets if there's no snow and the wind blows right through fleece. What can I do? I can't make them wear their winter jackets. I can't make them do anything. You can't make *anybody* do anything, I've figured that much out.

The other day I set an example by wearing my own warm clothes — a black crushed velvet cape, 1930s, that I got on eBay. It looks like the one Lombard wore to Jean Harlow's funeral in June in Los Angeles. Maybe hers wasn't lined. This one smells of sandalwood incense. They burn incense in lots of vintage clothing shops to keep the old clothes smell down. Me, I find that old clothes smell intoxicating. When I smell it, I know I'm someplace I want to be. Then again, I dream about finding great vintage stuff in shops. More than once I've dreamt about finding a black beaded twenties gown with a spray of bugle beads at the neckline. Does that mean I'll find it someday?

∞

The first time I saw a Carole Lombard movie was on a date, the one and only date I've been on. This guy Mitch that I worked with, he was really cool. He was into old movies, knew all about them, could always suggest the best one when someone came into the store looking for one. We had a lot of fun on shift together. Then he quit, got another job, and I was kind of sorry to see him go. But he came back one afternoon when I was working.

"There's a screwball comedy festival on at The Plaza right now," he said.

"A what festival?"

"Come on, screwball comedy. 1930s stuff, you know. *Bringing Up Baby*, *It Happened One Night*, *His Girl Friday*."

"Oh, yeah. Right."

"So, *Nothing Sacred*'s on tomorrow night. Do you want to go?"

"Sure."

Mom wanted to know where I was going. Even before the stroke, she always tried to make me feel bad about going out, even just for a few hours. I was stupid, I didn't think about it that time when she asked me. But I didn't know she was going to make such a big deal about it. When I told her I was going out to a movie with my friend Mitch, she lost it.

"You didn't ask my permission."

"I didn't know I had to. I'm nineteen."

"You still live in my house. You're still my daughter. Who is this Mitch?"

"A guy I work with."

She wanted to know what movie we were going to, what we were doing after the movie, what time we'd be back. I thought of asking her if she wanted to come with us, but I could see she wasn't in the mood for kidding around. She rarely was.

The movie was hilarious. Over a beer after Mitch entertained me with trivia about the director, William Wellman, who said Lombard was the only woman he'd ever known who could say four-letter words and make it come out poetry. I was home later than I'd told Mom, who still stirred around, coughing. I heard her bed squeak self-righteously. She gave me the cold shoulder for a while after that. Then a few days later I came home from work and found her on the kitchen floor.

∽

Travis and Noely and I used to go to the mall or the park or out for lunch on school PD days. Then all of a sudden, I don't know if it was their ages or what, but all they wanted to do was fight with each other on days off school. Sometimes, it took me all weekend to recover.

Last time the weather was nasty, too. So I had it planned out. Luckily there's no shortage of audio-visual equipment in the Martin household. We went down to the video store and picked out two movies each: Travis got *Ice Age* and *Lilo and Stitch*, Noely got *Cinderella* and *Beauty and the Beast II*. I got *No Man of Her Own* and *To Be or Not to Be*, Lombard's last film, released after the plane crash. Apparently she didn't even

Nothing Sacred

want to go on that War Bonds tour, but Gable felt his wife's career could use some propping up and insisted she go. Yikes.

So we were set. A movie each for the morning, another for the afternoon. The kids both have DVD players in their rooms and I used the one in the family room. We stopped and had a break for lunch, went for a walk, the two of them bitching about the cold the entire time. Then we got another movie rolling after lunch.

I dozed off in the middle of *To Be or Not to Be*, even though it's a funny movie. But I've seen it before. The credits rolled when I woke and looked out the window at the big, wet feathery flakes falling. I turned on a few lights, realized it was almost five, and Shelley would be home any minute. That was when I went upstairs and found Travis and Noely were gone.

∽

I leave the doors unlocked in case they come back while I'm out looking, then I flip on my cell and back my car out of the garage. The snow falls faster, thicker. Visibility is poor, the roads are slick. No kids at the playground. Traffic's a little heavier than usual right now, with people coming home. I feel a twinge of nausea thinking about how easy it would be to miss two little kids who've never crossed streets by themselves and maybe have no idea where they're going. They aren't at the school playground, either.

I try a few stores at the strip mall: Mac's, the Dairy Queen, the hardware store. No one has seen them. I run back to the car, head spinning, wet ropes of hair stuck to my face. I'm on the verge of tears but try to keep my mind clear, try to push down the little voice in my head that screams uncontrollably.

What can I do next, what can I do? I take a few deep breaths, then I decide to go back to the house. If they haven't come back, I'll call 911.

As I pull up, the two of them cross the street. They're not holding hands, as they've been taught, but walk five feet apart. Both of them have bags from Mac's, full of candy. Shelley stands in the doorway, I notice. I wonder how long she's been home.

I jump out of the car and pull them both toward me, gulp in air for a few seconds. It seems like I can't get enough, like I maybe forgot to breathe that whole time, maybe twenty minutes altogether, that I didn't know where they were. It seemed like hours. I stand back and now Shelley has her arms around them both. She's awfully quiet. I guess it must have been pretty strange for her to come home and find the doors unlocked and no one here and all.

"We went to the store, Ginny! Look," Noely says, letting me peer in at the Push Pops in her bag.

"We took all our allowance. And we didn't want to wake you up," Travis adds helpfully.

"You two go into the house, now," Shelley tells them. She's in the doorway now, blocking it, her steely gaze stares me down.

"Can you imagine those two? Going all that way by themselves? I guess I just dozed off for a few minutes and look what happened."

But Shelley won't answer, she won't even look at me. What does she want? Everything's fine, isn't it?

Art is Long

ONE NIGHT IN SEPTEMBER, SIX OF US were on a triple date at Night Magic, of all places. We tried to make it sound better, called it a bar, a dance club. But it was really a disco. It was okay, though, it didn't matter. Funny, really, a bunch of punk rockers going to a disco. I don't know whose idea it was. I bet Tina's husband thought it sounded romantic: ooh, Night Magic.

My friend Celia and I had just returned to Calgary from Vancouver. The Kinks were on their 1981 comeback tour and we caught their show at the PNE, and hit some shops. At Cabbages and Kinx I bought a pair of flat-heeled black leather knee-high boots, police or military surplus probably. I wore those, a pair of black jeans with a narrow red tartan belt and a black cavalry-style shirt with the buttons over to the left side. And some rhinestone earrings, nothing fancy. You, as I recall, wore jeans and a black T-shirt. You had shaved and your blond hair was still damp when I arrived. Oh my, your eyes ran up and down me, and stopped a long time at those boots.

"Hi, Matt," I'd said.

"Uh, hi, Julia. Nice boots."

I was on top of the world that night. For one thing, I'd just finished my first week at Alberta College of Art. Sure, the eight AM-to-five PM classes and several hours of homework nightly intimidated me a little, as did the sixty percent first-year dropout rate, but I was still excited about it. Even better, there I was on a date with you at last. You were older than me and you and your band, The Skullfuckers, intimidated me a little, but something about you had gripped me since I first met you. Something I didn't understand, couldn't analyze or even explain. I could only react. Now we were on a date at a disco, you buying me Zombies while music throbbed and pounded, your long legs tangling with mine under the table (we didn't dance). I noticed the gold flecks in your irises. That's quite a date drink, yes indeed, the old Zombie.

Not that I needed even one. God, how I wanted you.

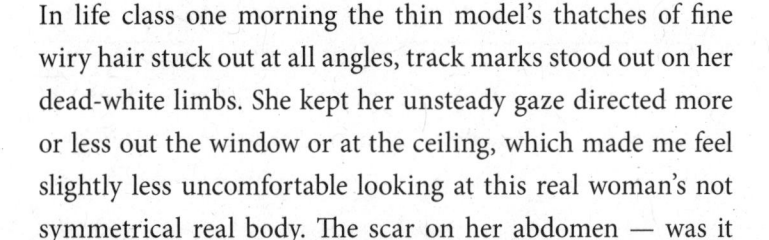

∾

In life class one morning the thin model's thatches of fine wiry hair stuck out at all angles, track marks stood out on her dead-white limbs. She kept her unsteady gaze directed more or less out the window or at the ceiling, which made me feel slightly less uncomfortable looking at this real woman's not symmetrical real body. The scar on her abdomen — was it from a c-section? It looked too far over to the side, though.

At lunchtime I slipped out before anyone could ask me to eat with them, listened to my shoes squeak on the hard snow on Fourteenth Street and lost myself in the crowd at the mall. I wandered around Sears in a fog of anxiety, looked at the facial creams for aging ladies at the cosmetics counter. Didn't I read some of these creams had some kind of hormones in them? What if I bought some and rubbed the whole jar on? Or ate it?

My friend Patsy told me she tried the hot bath and gin thing once. She said all that happened was that she fell asleep and had a hangover the next day. She still had to have an abortion.

Right then I guessed all I could do was wait. Well, wait and worry.

༄

"You are a Creator," our Perceptual Drawing instructor intoned. "Don't forget that. You have an important role in society. You are the intermediary between the Eternal and the Mortal." Some of his works hung on the walls of the lecture hall behind him. They looked like single crooked ink lines down the middle of really expensive pieces of rag paper to me, but what did I know?

"Speaking of roles, Julia," Dana whispered, "let's get out of here and roll a joint. This guy's a bore." Dana was from Brooks and her parents were not impressed she was at ACA. They wanted her to go to Olds Agricultural College, just like my parents wanted me to go to secretarial school.

"Not right now," I whispered back, though I really would have rather done that. I didn't come here for a bullshit lecture on How to Be an Artist, I thought. I just want to draw. And I will use a ruler.

༄

I couldn't sleep well right then. Every sound seemed magnified, and I hated listening to my roommate Debbie and her boyfriend Pete in the next bedroom. Even if they were just snoring, I didn't want to listen.

One night I walked to the 7-Eleven, the only place open, to look at magazines. The pale, pimply-faced guy behind the counter looked stoned, flipped through *Penthouse*, listened to reggae with headphones. I heard the bass line all the way over at the other end of the store. I could have stood there and read every magazine cover to cover and he wouldn't have noticed. I picked up the December *Dell Horoscopes*, read your monthly forecast, then mine. We weren't supposed to get along at all, you know. You're a man and I'm a woman, sure, but that just wasn't enough. Look what we were up against: you're an air sign, I'm a water sign. You're a fixed sign, I'm a cardinal sign. You're a cusp, too. And I'm an oldest child, you're a middle. This wasn't supposed to work at all, I knew that.

Dell Horoscopes pissed me off. I left after I bought some smokes from Peter Tosh. *Thanks, mon.*

∞

Harold Bell was our instructor in 3-D Design. A chain-smoking, snarly, unshaven little man, he had a reputation. The older students told us first years how we'd hate 3-D Design and how we'd hate Harry. They were right. I disliked him the first time I walked by his office. On a shelf right across from the doorway sat an industrial-sized mayonnaise jar with an inch or so of white glue, or something that looked like white glue, in it. "Harry's Sperm Bank" was scrawled in marker on a piece of masking tape across the front. Ha ha. I wondered how many years he'd been saving up.

Art Is Long

And his classes. The first thing he got us to do was cut out and fold and glue together fifty 1"x1"x1" white pyramids out of illustration board which we were to then mount into an "interesting arrangement" on black display board. After a while he gave us something a little more challenging to work on at home. He gave us each a hundred pieces of thin foot-long wooden doweling, something along the dimensions of Pick-Up Stix. With these we were to use white glue (Harry's favourite substance) to build a structure measuring no more than fifty centimetres in circumference that could support a one kilo brick for one minute. Extra marks if we used less than the allotted hundred sticks. We had a month to work on it before presenting it in class.

What is this, I thought, Toothpick Engineering 101?

But I couldn't let it worry me much. I had more important things on my mind.

༄

I didn't want anybody to hear me call the clinic, so I called from school early one morning. I got there at 7:30, headed to a pay phone. I looked at the bare concrete walls around me as I waited on hold. For an art college, that place had no soul. It looked more like Alberta Maximum Security Institution of Art. Then, of course as soon as they answered, a lineup suddenly appeared for the phone.

"Uh, yes," I said, turning around. "I'd like to make an appointment for a test."

"What kind of test?"

Shit. "A — well, a test."

"We do all kinds of tests. What kind do you want?"

"A pregnancy test," I said quietly.
"A pregnancy test, you said?"
"Yes."
"I see. How late are you?"
"A week."
"We can't do it if you're only a week late."
"You can't?"
"No. You have to be at least a month late for the test to produce any results."
"Oh."
"But I can make an appointment for you to come in later."
"No. Thanks. Never mind."

Maybe I imagined it, but it seemed to me that everybody standing in line behind me smirked as I walked past them. Fuck them, let them smirk.

∾

"Hey, Julia. Anything happen yet?" Debbie asked when I got home that night.

"Nope. Nothing yet."

"Don't worry. Whatever happens, you'll work it out."

"Looks like I'll have to work it out by myself. Why doesn't he call?"

"Because he's an asshole. And he's terrified. Pete told him — I hope you don't mind."

"No. He should know."

I didn't know what I'd do. I couldn't have an abortion. It wasn't the Church; I didn't give a shit about the Church and I didn't believe in heaven and hell and all that. But I just could not do it. I wouldn't be able to live with the guilt, I was sure. So what then? Marry you? Right. You couldn't commit to anything, not a job, not a girlfriend, not a pet goldfish. I guessed I'd have to drop out of school, get a job. Who'd look after the baby? Maybe I'd have to give it up for adoption. That would probably be the best thing. But it would kill me.

And then I didn't have to worry anymore. On a dark, grey day at the beginning of December, my period started. Hallelujah. Never before had I been so happy to be on the rag.

∽

Just before classes ended at Christmas we presented our brick-supporting structures in Harry's class. They all failed dismally. Mine, like most of them, used all one hundred sticks and the brick stayed in the air for about a second. I got a C minus, like most of us did. Harry watched almost silently, jotting in his ledger beside our names as one by one our projects crashed. After the last one, he paced the front of the room and glared at us for a long, terrible minute. Then he told us we had no imaginations and we should look for jobs over the holidays, because there was no point in any of us hanging around an art college. One student who used a hundred and fifty sticks and whose brick stayed in the air for thirty seconds did better, got a C. Another who glued together just enough sticks to hold the brick up for a split second, only about twenty, got a B minus. His structure got flattened right away, but he didn't use many sticks.

As I dragged my portfolio and books onto the bus to go home I wondered what we learned from this. That the best way to approach a project is to do the least amount of work possible? That some people will ask you to do impossible things? That sometimes things will crash, no matter what we do?

Or maybe it was just that Harry was a giant asshole.

A couple of days after we returned from Christmas break I decided to drop out of ACA. I just got up in the middle of a class and cleaned out my locker and left.

I felt so free.

∾

Life is weird. After all these years, it turns out you're an artist now. Celia told me she'd heard you were a waiter, but that just shows you what she knows. You were back in town from Toronto for a while last spring and we went for a drink, got caught up. We hadn't seen each other in more than twenty years and I was a little nervous about the whole thing. I didn't know what to wear. A few weeks earlier I'd happened to come across my old Vancouver boots in a box in the basement and thought about wearing them. But then I decided not to.

I spotted you in the bar right away. You looked much the same, maybe a little heavier, a little hairier. I hoped you weren't thinking the same thing about me. Conversation was easy, and before long you started talking about your paintings.

"I had no idea you were interested in visual art. What happened to music?" I asked.

"I drifted away from music a long time ago. It stopped being fun. I guess art is something I got started in later in life. But Van Gogh was what, twenty-seven when he started painting?"

"He was also a genius. And you're forty-five."

Art Is Long

"True. I guess I've just always felt an urge to be creative, you know. To be a creator, that's a cool feeling."

"Sure. So where can I see some of your stuff?"

"Oh, I've been in some shows in Toronto. Don't think you can see anything online right now. I'll e-mail you some slides." I knew you wouldn't.

"What about a day job?" I asked.

"I'm in public service. In the restaurant trade. Pays the bills, you know."

I smiled, thought of Celia. "Of course."

"So I hear you're married," you said. "I hear you have kids. Tell me about them."

"Well, my husband, Jake, is a geologist. Used to be a musician but he grew up and got a job. We've been together twenty years, been married for fifteen. And then Max and Ian are ten and eight. They're a lot of fun. Max plays piano and Ian's into sports. They both really like the Ramones. All kids do." I dug around in my purse and found my wallet. "Here's a picture." Showing you a picture of my kids felt weird, I have to say.

"Cute kids. They look like you."

"Funny you say that. People usually say they look like Jake. You know, things are so different since we had them. Better different. I can't imagine my life without them. What about you? No wives, no kids?"

You laughed. "Nope, none. Well, I had a close call a little while ago. A girlfriend of mine had to have an abortion."

"Oh, Matt."

"Yeah. At least I know I'm not shooting blanks."

Shooting blanks? How could you kid about that? I shuddered, remembering how I felt just having to consider it, not even actually going through it like this girl did. And now it was just cocktail conversation, and she was how many girls ago?

Before long it was time for me to pick up the kids from school. We left the bar and you crushed me against your grey wool coat. We said goodbye and I watched you walk away down the street and around the corner. As I walked to my car, waves of feeling fought to come to the surface — anger, sadness, relief, regret, pity, I couldn't tell what all — before crashing down around me. The hell of it was that in spite of everything, part of me still wanted you. Was it the flecks in your irises that I noticed again? Maybe it was just the memory of being young that seemed attractive.

But what did it matter now? Forget it, I told myself. It was all a long time ago.

I know one thing. If I ever see you again, I'll bring you a mayonnaise jar.

We Had Faces Then

I EAT MY LUNCH IN THE STAFF room, being careful not to get anything on the pages of this new book, *Hurrell's Hollywood Portraits* by Mark A. Viera. I love his books. I had his last one, *Sin in Soft Focus: Pre-Code Hollywood*, out for ages until some joker put a hold on it. The nerve. This one's been on order for months, but it's finally here, and it's worth the wait. They're all in here: Joan Crawford, Jean Harlow, Errol Flynn, Greta Garbo, Marlene Dietrich, Rita Hayworth, Cary Grant, Carole Lombard, Clark Gable, Gloria Swanson. *We had faces then.* The pages are stiff, glossy, still smell of printer's ink. Hurrell was big into shadows, so the whole range of tones from the raven's wing black of Hedy Lamarr's hair to the talcum powder white of Anna May Wong's cheekbones, and every in-between of the grey scale all reach out, mesmerize me. Part of the endless fascination for me in these photos is wondering where the real face ends and the art begins. Let's face it, you and I have never seen a live human being that looks like these lush art deco portraits of Robert Taylor or Norma Shearer. Not even Robert Taylor or Norma Shearer looked that much like them. Sometimes I can't decide whether it's fascinating or frightening.

A wave of nausea takes me by surprise and I run to the ladies' room. When I come back I hear Joan from Circulation say, not quite under her breath, "Hey, you'd be sick too, if you had to have tofu for lunch." Joan's such a card. You don't hear me remarking on that white bread, fibre-free, processed mystery meat thing she calls a sandwich, do you? But of course, I just smile.

⁓

When you work in a library, you think a lot about the great chain of being. Or the great chain of reading, at least. My own chain is endless; I'm always adding new and sometimes surprising links. Sometimes I wonder, am I the sum of my interests, the sum of the tangents I go off on? Do they define me as much as I define them? Sometimes it seems like I don't have any choice in the matter. I'll get swept up in something, start reading about it, and it leads to something else. The piles of books on my coffee table, in my locker, beside my bed grow and grow and grow and I just barely seem able to keep up with them. I often think that if I could somehow quit my job I'd have a lot more time to read.

I'll give you one little example from the chain. I had this boyfriend, Sam, many years ago. In retrospect, I guess you could barely even call him a boyfriend, really. Let's just say we were involved briefly. Anyway, he turned me on to Billie Holiday and, some years later when Sam was just a bad memory, I read her memoir, *Lady Sings the Blues*. Of course, she didn't really write it herself. The byline on the cover says,

We Had Faces Then

"As told to William Dufty". It was fascinating, well-written, so I read another book of Dufty's called *Sugar Blues*. The dedication in this one reads "For Billie Holiday, whose death changed my life, and Gloria Swanson, whose life changed my death". All right, I'm a bit of a movie freak, I know who Gloria Swanson was, obviously. She was the hugest star of the silent era, next to Mary Pickford.

But I wanted to know what the connection was between the writer, the actress, and the singer. It turns out Gloria Swanson, a long-time vegetarian and health food enthusiast, met Dufty and got him off of sugar, caffeine, alcohol, and tobacco and onto a macrobiotic diet. And he realized after writing a book about a junkie, what a junkie he was himself, what junkies so many of us are, without even realizing it. A year after *Sugar Blues* was published Dufty married Swanson, who was seventeen years older than him, becoming the last of her six husbands. I couldn't help thinking of *Sunset Boulevard*. He was also the ghost writer on her autobiography, *Swanson on Swanson*, which came out a couple of years before her death. She lived to be eighty-four and he lived to be eighty-six, so I started to think there must be something to this diet. Then I read up on macrobiotics, but it sounded too weird. Since then, though, I haven't eaten any meat and I've cut way back on the caffeine, and I feel a lot better.

And back to the chain of being, I guess all that never would have happened if it hadn't been for Sam and his Billie Holiday records. He's left me a legacy he could never even imagine. As I recall, he wasn't much on books. It was just not meant to be.

Actually, I recently reread parts of *Swanson on Swanson*. I wanted to be sure I remembered it right. Swanson had an abortion in the twenties that she always regretted, even up to the end of her life. You wouldn't think someone that rich and famous could regret something that long. You wouldn't think it could stay with you like that. But there you go.

∽

The people at work resemble a big, dysfunctional family. We kid about it, in an uneasy way. We've all been there far too long, for one thing. We bitch and complain about the cutbacks and staffing levels and reorganization and automation, but we're mostly still all here. And it's more than just the fact that most of us are liberal arts people who aren't really qualified for much else. A lot of us are people who have to be around books. Junkies, you might say.

My mother comes in the second Saturday of every month and we go out for lunch, always to the same little café across the street. Mom always orders a Black Forest ham sandwich with fries. And she always has to get in some little dig about whatever I order. "Has that got enough protein in it, Marian?"

The first time she came to have lunch with me, I was excited about my new job and spent quite a while talking about it. Mom was only half-listening, I could soon tell, and then finally she asked me what I was getting paid. I told her.

"Mitchell Givens, Susan's boy, just started his job and he makes twice that."

"Well, he's an engineer."

"He went to school for four years. You went to school for four years."

I looked out the window at the people walking by, at the library across the street, tried not to think about choking her.

We Had Faces Then

I wanted to tell her to get off my back. I wanted to ask her what her big career was. I wanted to tell her to fuck off. But I just sat there with a tight-lipped smile on my face. Like I always do, like I still do.

She's dropped that now, the cracks about money. Up until a year ago she was after me to get married, even asked me if there was something wrong that I didn't seem interested in men. But I guess she concluded that I was probably too old to have a baby now, so she doesn't talk about it anymore. I guess that was the only reason she wanted me to get married.

∽

You think about a lot of other things, too, when you work in a library. Some people think they have an idea of what it's like, especially people who rarely, or never, go into libraries. They think we sit and read all the books that come in, and help cherub-faced children and sweet little old ladies find books, and that it's quiet and peaceful. We do help people find books, but a lot of other things go on, too. Besides information work, I mean. The reality of most urban downtown libraries is that, more than ever, they are refuges for those who have nowhere else to go. Libraries have always been havens for the homeless, drunks, the mentally ill, the junkies, the plain old eccentric, the lonely. It's different now than it was when I started, though. There are more people in this city now, for one thing, and fewer places for the fringe people to go.

There's also a different kind of junkie around these days. Crackheads are all over the place now, and they're scary. They're twitchy, irrational, and often out of control. They're also desperate, and they steal purses and backpacks. Used to be flashers worried a lot of the staff (myself, I always just laugh at them). Now we've got to keep the doors to non-public areas locked at all times. People complain about the needles in the public washrooms. A little while ago someone from Periodicals saw a woman try to shoot herself up *in the eye* in the washroom downstairs. We had a skeletal twenty-year-old junkie drop to the floor and die of heart failure right in front of the Social Sciences desk last month.

The point is, I'm scared of these people now, and I never used to be. Live and let live I always figured. Now I'm not so sure. You can't reason with crackheads, and you never know what they'll do. And somehow, before, I used to be able to consider them as individuals, with their own problems, their own set of circumstances that led them to, say, crouching over the index table staring at nothing and talking rapid-fire and incomprehensibly to themselves, while gripping a historical atlas of Eastern Europe in their shaking hands. Or whatever they might be doing. Now they've become faceless to me, the enemy, almost. Sometimes when I work nights, I'm scared shitless as I wait for the bus home. That never used to happen to me.

Of course, maybe I'm just getting old, like my mother says. I guess there's that, too.

∽

I stayed after the library was closed one night. It was a Saturday, and we'd been really busy, so I didn't get a chance to work on a report I was supposed to finish for Monday morning. But before I got into it, I wanted to look at the new Hurrell book we had in the reference collection. After all, I wasn't in any particular rush to get home.

As I walked over to my desk in the workroom, I thought about how funny it is that people think libraries are quiet. During open hours, they're anything but quiet with people talking, cell phones ringing, kids squalling. But even when the building is closed, when all the people are gone, it's never completely quiet. The fluorescent lights hum, there's the noise from the heating system, the computers, sounds of traffic outside. I made myself a coffee and before long I was absorbed in two full-page studies of Bette Davis' face. The lighting is intentionally overexposed in these pictures so that you see the pores in her chalk-white skin, you see every eyebrow hair, every eyelash. Her expression is serene, almost dreamy or drowsy, and yet I found something about these portraits disturbing, intrusive.

Then I felt the hand on my shoulder.

I still don't understand where he came from. Not that there aren't all kinds of places he could hide in here: behind unlocked doors, in the stairwells, behind the stacks in some places. All he'd have to do is keep his eyes on the staff when they were doing the final check, and stay out of their line of vision. Suddenly, he was standing there and I had no clue, no warning at all.

∾

For weeks afterward, I pored through old incident reports, going back years. Nothing, no mention of him anywhere. Which means nothing really, just that he's never had a run-in with anyone before, or if he has there's no paper trail. I tried to imagine what my report of this particular incident would look like.

DESCRIPTION OF SUBJECT: *Male, Caucasian, 6'1", 200 lbs., beard, long dark hair, black coat.*

DESCRIPTION OF INCIDENT: *Subject entered workroom after hours and assaulted lone staff member.*

ACTION TAKEN: *Staff member was shocked into a state of inertia for some time after the incident took place, trying to figure out whether the whole thing had really happened or not. She didn't finish the new Hurrell book or her report. She went home and had a shower and didn't sleep very well.*

For a while I toyed with the idea of telling someone. But who? My supervisor? The police? In one way, it seemed like the right thing to do. Even if it was too late for me, it might save someone else. But I couldn't see what good it would do me now. And it seemed like a lot of bad things could happen. People would talk, for one thing. Word gets around this place like wildfire. They'd talk about how stupid I was to be here after hours by myself. About how I didn't have the sense to fight back. And it happened so fast. I barely got a good look at him, really, weird as that sounds. I know the big details, but I'm a little foggy on his face. Most of all, I didn't want to talk about it. I just couldn't make myself do it.

I vaguely remember, in my dazed state, saying goodnight to the security guard when I did eventually leave, and wondered on the bus home whether he'd seen the man leave. Maybe he was still there. While it was happening, I kept thinking if only I could reach a phone, I could call security. And after he left

We Had Faces Then

the workroom I could have called, maybe I should have. But I didn't. I couldn't. For a long time I was just curled up on the carpet where he left me. I never noticed before that the baseboards in the workroom were so dusty. Were they like that all over the building? Someone should really tell maintenance about that, I thought.

∽

A lot of those movie stars were funny about babies. About wanting to have them, I mean. Apparently, Jean Harlow's fondest desire was to marry and have a family. Marilyn Monroe was devastated by her repeated miscarriages and much has been written about the irony of the sex goddess unable to have a child of her own. Joan Crawford adopted. A lot of movie stars ended up adopting. Even Mary Pickford, the first movie star, America's Sweetheart. It wouldn't be because they'd had one too many abortions. And then there were all those stars who managed to remain mysteriously childless, even back in the pre-Pill days. Gloria Swanson is the only star I've ever heard of who regretted it, who even had the courage to admit she had one. And then to have the courage to admit she regretted it — amazing. But then, it wasn't something people used to talk about.

They still don't, when you come right down to it.

∽

Do you have to go through your worst fear to be released from it? That can't really be true, not always. But it seems to have happened for me, in this case. Has the worst happened? I believe things happen for a reason; sometimes the reason isn't always obvious. Sometimes you have to think about it for a while. And then if you still don't see the reason, you have to leave it alone, stop thinking about it. Sooner or later, the reason will unfold itself.

∽

I sit in my corner of the staff room having supper and hoping Joan comes in so I can give her a taste of my tempeh curry. Just for a change I'm reading a book, off on a new tangent this time. *What to Expect When You're Expecting*, a classic in its genre, is in its third edition with more than ten million copies sold. And you can see why; it's an informative book for people who have a million and one questions about what will happen to them in the coming months.

At first I thought I didn't dare risk putting holds on pregnancy books. I worried that people would talk. The Circulation staff would find out, and it would spread from there. So at first, I just read what we had on the shelf, but I soon discovered all the good books were out all the time, so it was either put holds on them or go broke buying them. The last couple of weeks I've been picking up my holds, and people have been offering their congratulations and asking when the baby is due. Nobody at work has asked me who the father is yet, although I'm sure that will come. Curiosity will get the best of someone sooner or later and the politeness and discretion will come to an end. That was the first thing my mother asked, who was the father. I have to say, I kind of enjoyed watching her round face go ashy white when I told her I didn't know.

And in the end, so what? So I'm having a baby, so I'll be away from work for a while. It happens every day. So the father

We Had Faces Then

is faceless to me. That happens, too. And if people don't like it, they can go fuck themselves. All I know for sure is, I have a lot to read in the next little while. How do you like that? I'll finally have my chance to be off work for a while, and I won't have any time to read. It figures.

Blue Lake

YOU PUT THE KEY IN THE LOCK and for a moment, I am afraid it won't work. It sticks, but then you pull on the door, covered with thick coats of checked cream paint, and it squeaks open. Inside, the little house seems very quiet, the torrent drums steadily on the roof. As my eyes adjust to the dark, the faded curtains patterned with tea roses glow dull yellow and pink.

Midafternoon is dark as night in the rain in the grove of whispering aspens. We should have known this would happen, with the banks of iron-coloured cloud that started to roll in around noon. We should have known, but we didn't pay any attention. Thunder rumbles in the distance. All the earlier heat has been drawn out of the day and now we stand in sock feet, drip on the rag rug in the doorway of this little house, and I am cold to the bone.

"I put some towels in the bedroom closet when I was here last week," you tell me. I feel around on the bedroom's floral patterned wallpaper until I find a light switch. I've taken off my socks and dry my face and hair, but still tremble. You come into the room with your arms full of firewood and newspaper. "We'll get the fire lit in here." Then I notice the little stove, maybe two feet tall, near the foot of the bed. Its door creaks as you open it. You crumple newspaper, throw on some thin, dry sticks of kindling, then the match.

"You know," you say, "you'll to have to get out of those wet clothes."

Of course, you're right. I hesitate. But then, this is no time to think, I tell myself as I hang my jeans, my sweater, my underwear, on the white painted bed railings. I towel off quickly while you poke and adjust logs, and then I slip under the covers: white flannelette sheets with blue stripes and red blanket stitching on the edges, and a faded chenille bedspread whose colours are now indistinguishable.

My breath is shallow, I realize, as I watch you, and I try to take deeper breaths. You look exactly the way I remember you, don't seem changed at all, and I wonder how this can be. I know I've changed. The smells of woodsmoke and wet clothes fill the little room. It seems to me you take a long time lighting the fire, and just as I start to feel uncomfortable, you stand and turn toward me and smile.

"Mind if I join you?"

"Not at all."

You begin to unbutton your shirt, when the room is lit by a flash, followed immediately by the tearing roar of thunder.

"That was close," I whisper, as though trying to keep my exact location from the lightning.

You towel off, hang your clothes beside mine, poke the now blazing fire and slide under the covers.

"Are you afraid?" you ask.

"Of the lightning?"

We lie and look at each other. Words shrink and die away, though there are so many in my mind, on my lips, in my heart. But they have waited all these years. They can wait a little longer. The chenille rises and falls over us, between us, in waves. Your breath warms my skin. Again, I feel as though I can't breathe enough. Then I feel your warm hand slide onto my waist and rest there. How can you not be cold, I wonder?

∽

I always stop in Red Deer for coffee because it's the halfway point on Highway 2 to Edmonton, right about the place you need to restart the bathroom / coffee cycle. But partly also because it's near Blue Lake. I haven't been to Blue Lake in many years, but I always see the signs on the highway.

This is one of those prairie summer days stuck in the storm cycle: sun and heat in the morning, which causes the previous night's moisture to evaporate, causing storm clouds, causing rain, which falls and evaporates by midafternoon. The cycle builds and builds.

It's crowded in the Horton's, everyone's covered in a thin film of sweat, and yet we drink hot coffee. An elderly man asks if he can sit at my table. "This is the kind of day we watch for funnel clouds," he says. The sky to the northeast, in the direction of Blue Lake, is a forbidding black. What if a tornado had swept you away when you were out there working, I wonder, before I understand the stupidity of this.

Blue Lake

The man continues. "My brother was out at Pine Lake that year, you know. He was okay. They got Doppler radar now, to tell us when there's a tornado on the way. But I don't see the point."

"Warns people," I suggest. "Gives them a chance to take shelter."

"Maybe," he concedes. "But part of life here is learning that you have to surrender to the elements sometimes."

∽

The cold draws out of me, gradually. The fire warms my feet, your hands move slowly over the rest of me. My hands find you: warm, still somehow familiar. The body must have a memory of its own. I remember things about you I didn't know I'd forgotten. Another flash, another sky-splitting crack. I wince. You pull me closer to you, your lips brush my ear. "Don't be afraid."

Afraid isn't the word for it, really.

∽

The bathroom looks different from the rest of the house. I can't really think of it as a cabin — to my mind, a cabin means logs — but I suppose that's what it is. The rectangular frosted glass light fixture, the squared-off edges of the sink, the vanity, even the toilet all remind me of a seventies apartment I used to live in. For such young guys, you did a pretty good job of building the bathroom, I have to say. I remember it took a long time, you and your brother coming up here weekends to do it. I always wanted to come with you, and do my best to prevent you from working. But you wouldn't ask me. And I couldn't ask you.

∽

One day, instead of stopping in Red Deer for coffee, I drive right to Blue Lake with a cup from the drive-thru. It's time now, it just feels like it. I have to see it again.

I drive up and down the road that runs along the shore of the lake a few times before I realize the cabin's no longer there. I think at first that I can't remember where it was, that I was only there once a long time ago. But I see now that it's gone. They're building vacation residences, crammed in beside each other all along this side of the lake. The trembling aspen are gone too. I could let this bother me; often, in the past, I have let things like this bother me. But I'm trying these days to be more accepting of things I can't change. I'm trying harder to let go because I know I can let things get drawn out, too drawn out.

I drive a little ways down the road to the public beach. It's not really beach season yet, there's just an elderly couple walking along the shore. Then again, it's midweek, too. The bulldozers and front-end loaders roar and crunch, make way for yet more placid get-away spots as I get out of the car and take my coffee over to a picnic table. I tune out the noise and focus on the glint of sunlight off the lake's surface.

∽

Once you and your brother were finished the bathroom, you threw a big party at the cabin. So I finally did get my invitation to Blue Lake. For some reason I could not fathom, the idea of being alone with you later really did it for me. The anticipation was almost more than I could stand.

We arrived late on a hot afternoon, and the thunderstorm building in the distance appeared to be not far behind. We roasted hot dogs in a firepit on the beach, drank beer until dusk fell.

I went inside to use the new bathroom, and wondered which parts you'd done. I'd hoped you'd follow me into the cabin; I wanted to put my plans into action. I stopped in the kitchen to talk to some people for a while, when your brother came in and asked me if I'd seen you. The last time I saw you, you sat by one of the firepits on the beach.

I went outside with him, down to the darkened beach. Some of the people who'd sat around the fire with you walked up and down the shore now, some waded into the water and a guy in a plaid shirt ran toward us.

∽

The fire dies down a little and you get up to tend it. I am tired, but also enervated. I notice a shelf on the wall across from the bed. Tin soldiers line up on it, marching nowhere.

"Whose soldiers?"

"My uncle's. Great-uncle's, actually, I guess. My family's been coming up here a long time."

I watch the soldiers' shadows flicker on the wall as the fire blazes up, then I drift off.

∽

I asked the guy in the plaid shirt where you were.

"He went in for a swim a while ago, and now we can't see him."

I felt a little sick, then. "It's dark," I said, as if no one had noticed.

"And he's really loaded," the guy added.

We split up to look for you. Soon everyone at the party searched while we waited for the Mounties to come, and we kept searching while they dragged the lake. It helped me, somehow, to hope that maybe you just came out of the lake unnoticed, that maybe you were off somewhere, reading a book, or sleeping or something. This hope was the only thing that enabled me to get any sleep at all, on the old couch in the cabin, under a faded chenille bedspread.

The thunderstorms never did materialize that night. I couldn't help but think that if they had, you might not have gone swimming. But the rain came in the morning, pocked the iron-grey surface of Blue Lake as your brother and I stood on the beach and sipped from mugs of strong coffee. We watched as the RCMP divers drew your dripping, naked body out of the lake. It seemed sudden, when it happened, even though the time had dragged all night, even though it was becoming obvious that this would happen. I don't know why it should have seemed sudden.

∞

You come up for air, from under chenille, and although I think by now that you must be exhausted, you surprise me again. And again. I find myself out of time, out of the world, in this little room. Nothing else is. This one little room has become an everywhere. Soon even the room disappears, the bed, the stove, the soldiers. All that is left is pure physical sensation; my body moves as one with yours. Where do you end and I begin? Right now, I could not say.

Slowly, my awareness returns to things outside of you and me. The fire, I notice, has gone out. The rain drums down very hard now. All is white light for a moment, followed by a huge crack of sound.

"I'm not afraid," I whisper, and you smile.

Rain in December

LOVE IS A GAMBLE, I KEEP TELLING myself. A risk. There's always the potential for rejection, for pain, when you love somebody. That's why, as my plane lands in Vancouver, doubt twists my stomach into knots. This was a stupid idea. I'm making a fool of myself. And there's no fool like an old fool, right?

It's only the beginning of December but already, people are going home to be with their families. They're throwing their arms around each other and it hurts to see them, unafraid to make big emotional scenes, as I wait for my suitcase to appear among the others circling at the luggage ramp. I can't help wishing Rosie were here to meet me.

Rosie — she's the reason I came out here. Lately, I've been thinking about those I've lost one way or another — my sister, Rosie, my husband Jim. I can't bring the other two back, but I can still try to make amends with Rosie.

It's been on my mind more than ever these last two years, since Jim's been gone. I still roll over in bed at night, expecting him to be there. It's not just that I'm lonely, now — which I

Rain In December

am. But when Jim died, I realized I won't live forever. And I have to see my baby again before I go.

So I'm reaching out to her once more. I have nothing to lose, the way I see it: if she's happy to see me, coming out here unannounced will have been a wonderful thing. If she slams the door in my face, I'm no worse off. It wouldn't be the first time I've had a little egg on my face. Those things don't seem so important, when you're my age. If she turns me away, I can stay with my brother Bill in White Rock.

Maybe before I get a cab, I'll have a coffee here at the airport. The flight from Regina seemed long, but not long enough, if you know what I mean. I need more time to consider what to say.

My sister's also been on my mind a lot the last little while. I was angry with her for a lot of years. Then came acceptance. Now I understand, I think, as much as anybody could. To this day, over twenty-five years later, I still wonder what was going through her mind.

∽

Rose was two years older than me, and she always seemed lucky. Evenings, Dad drove cab and Mom made cabbage rolls, ironed, mended. I was stuck doing homework at the kitchen table.

"Alice, get that, would you?" Mom would yell at me when an awkward, stammering boy phoned or showed up at the door for Rosie. Rosie was usually getting ready for a date with someone else so she'd get me to stall, make excuses, lie for her. I would have been happy to go out with some of her leftovers. Dates were few and far between for me. Like all the

Chumka women, we were both big, but Rosie had delicate features, smooth, pale skin, almond-shaped grey eyes and thick chestnut hair. She looked like Mom as a girl; I looked like Dad. I had his blond hair, ruddy complexion, lumpy nose. She was outgoing; I was shy. I hated it, wished I could be like her.

She'd been out of high school a little over a year when she got engaged to Stan Woloczsin, and I figured she had it made. She planned to quit her job at Kresge's (Stan made good money at the potash plant) and stay home with the babies. It sounded great to me.

We didn't realize anything was wrong until the wedding. Rosie's face looked a little grey, but we thought it was just nerves. They made it through the ceremony, signed the papers, but she dropped to the floor like somebody had pulled her knees out from under her just before we set up the receiving line.

Stan and Bill carried her out to Stan's car and they rushed her to the Grey Nuns. Mom and Dad and I followed in Bill's car, but by the time we got there she was already in one of the examining rooms with Stan. After what seemed like forever, he emerged ashen-faced, looked sick himself now. His tux was wrinkled, the boutonniere was crushed and limp.

"Well," asked Mom. "What did the doctor say?"

"She's in labour," he said quietly, unable to meet Mom's eyes.

After that, none of us spoke for a long time. I'm amazed Mom didn't get hysterical, Dad didn't try to kill him. She hadn't looked pregnant. I guess it was just the way she carried the baby. I knew she'd never been regular, but in nine months you'd think she'd have noticed something. Then again, I've heard of women who didn't miss a period all the way through pregnancy. She didn't mention any morning sickness, any cravings. Maybe she had them, and chalked it up to other things.

"Can you believe how she's humiliated us?" Dad said on the way home from the hospital.

"That's what you're worried about?" Mom hissed. "What people will think about you? Who cares what they think?"

"Look, everything's going to be okay," I said and leaned toward the front seat, hoping to avert a full-blown battle in the car. Dad's driving was erratic enough without distractions. "The doctor said she'll be fine. She has a beautiful, healthy little girl. So, they got an early start on things. They're married. Maybe only a few hours before the baby was born, okay, but they're married."

Mom looked at me over her shoulder, then turned to Dad. "What she says makes sense, Ivan."

"I'm glad one of our daughters makes sense."

People would talk for a while. Sure, it was embarrassing, but it would blow over eventually. We could have laughed it off, I'm sure of it even now.

Rose seemed numb the next day. She didn't talk much, didn't seem to notice us, or her baby. The nurse told us she hadn't eaten. Mom sat and held her hand while she stared out the window. She was still in shock and exhausted. The doctor said a little rest would help.

The next morning I went to see her alone. Mom and Dad planned to come in the afternoon. Her doctor waited at the nurses' station to see me. He took me into an empty office near Rosie's room. I can still see the sun glinting off his wire-rimmed glasses as he spoke to me.

He spoke gently, slowly, deliberately. "Your parents are on their way here. This morning when one of the nurses brought the baby into your sister's room, she found Rosie dead. She hung herself in the closet with a bed sheet."

I tuned out after that, didn't hear anything else he said, could only hear the blood pound in my ears, could only think of that poor baby. Jim and I were never able to have kids of our own, so I don't really know what it's like, but I've heard that post-partum depression is terrible. Maybe that's what happened. Better that than dying of embarrassment.

We brought little Rosie home. Mom and Dad became her legal guardians, which I think was a relief to Stan. He feebly suggested he could do it alone, but Mom convinced him it would be better to leave her with us. Having the baby around forced us to put aside sadness, anger, and just get on with things. Stan came to visit often, at first. He tried, but his discomfort meant it was soon only weekends, then less frequently — holidays, her birthday. Rosie was almost two when Stan remarried and moved to Winnipeg. She had as much family as a baby needed and he needed to start over. They became Uncle Stan and Aunt Beverley who sent Christmas presents and birthday cards.

Although Mom and Dad were her guardians, almost from the time we brought her home it felt to me like Rosie was mine. I fed her, changed her, bathed her, played with her when I wasn't at school. I graduated a few months after she was born and then fell into being a mom full-time. Still, I found time to fall in love with Jim.

Rain In December

Rosie was almost three when we married. By then I was so attached to her that I couldn't leave her with Mom and Dad, so we adopted her. If my sister had been sterile instead of me, so much would have been different. Life is so strange.

∽

Another coffee, and maybe a sandwich, while I'm here. That in-flight meal wasn't fit for a dog. Besides, what's the rush? Nobody's expecting me.

Looking back, I think telling Rosie the truth was a mistake. Saying nothing would have been a lot easier. That was why it took me so long to get around to telling her the strange, sad story of her first days in this world. But I owed it to her, and to my sister, to tell the truth. I figured if I didn't tell her, somebody else would. The story had travelled and while it had happened long ago, enough people knew. Someone without her best interests at heart, who didn't care how much the truth hurt, could devastate her with a single sentence.

I tried to put it as simply as I could. "This is very hard for me to say. It's something I've wanted to tell you for years. I'm not really your mother, not your biological mother. I'm really your Aunt Alice. Auntie Rosie was your mother."

She didn't say much, just sat there and nodded. Looking, at that moment, so much like Rosie I wondered if she didn't already have an idea. I told her about the wedding, her birth, Rosie's suicide. She looked so calm, so unaffected, that I started to wonder if what I said was sinking in.

"Do you understand all of this?" I finally asked.

"Yes," she answered. "But why didn't you tell me before? Why did you wait until I was almost twenty?"

She made it sound like I'd waited until she'd reached an advanced age. "I wanted to tell you before. I've wanted to tell you for years, but I didn't know how you'd react."

I knew it was a lot for her to take in all at once, but I didn't know how to make it easier for her. At first she seemed to accept it, but as the weeks went by she became distant. She stayed away from the house more and more, and when she was home, hardly said a word. It threw me; I was prepared for anger, I was prepared for sadness. I wasn't prepared for silence. About six months later she moved to Vancouver. She'd talked about leaving Regina for ages. Even as a little girl she always said she'd move someplace warm when she grew up. I don't know if finding out the truth was what made her go, but maybe it helped her to make up her mind.

I stood in her bedroom doorway as she packed and asked if she wanted to talk about her mother.

"No. I'm not stuck in the past the way you are. I've dealt with it. What's there to talk about?"

The only time she came back to Regina was for Jim's funeral. Even then, she was cold, distant, stayed overnight and left the next morning. Now she never phones and when I call her, she just answers 'yes' and 'no', sounds busy. Birthday and Christmas cards are signed "Love, Rosie," but no note, no letter.

It hurts. Some days I wish I'd never brought the whole thing up. But I had to. She'll come around eventually, but it's been five years and when I suggest coming out here she's always busy, always finds an excuse. This time, if she wants to reject me, she'll have to do it to my face.

Rain In December

Finally, it's time to get a cab. I've never been to Vancouver before, have no idea where the driver's taking me. He's chatty and while I'm not really in a talkative mood, it takes my mind off the scene ahead. I marvel at the weather: of course, I'd always heard they didn't get snow in Vancouver, but I didn't expect to see green grass or leaves on the trees. Regina was twenty below when I left only a few hours ago. This seems like a small miracle.

"Here we are," he says, and stops in front of a white stucco bungalow. I pay the fare, he offers to carry my suitcase in for me. I decline. She lives in the main floor suite of this house. I try to remind myself to smile as I advance up the front walk, know that nervousness has made my jaw set so that I look stern, older. I reach the top step and set my suitcase down; it feels heavier now than it did at the airport. The rain has started, and now I must ring the bell, or risk looking like an old fool, standing in the rain with my suitcase. I still can't get over it — rain in December. I take a deep breath and ring the bell.

No answer. I feel a strange sense of relief and breathe out. She's not home. Of course, having come all this way I'd be foolish to ring only once. Confident it will produce no results, I press the buzzer again. This time I hear feet pad toward the entrance. She opens the door and meets my eyes with a short, sharp gasp, looks much the same as she did two years ago, like a thin version of my sister. I am obviously the last person she expected. I try, I try, to read her expression for that long silent moment we stand and stare at each other. Will she be sullenly polite and invite me in out of a sense of duty? Before I know it, she's wrapped her arms around me, as far as she can get them around me, that is, in a bear hug. She pulls back and looks at me with wet almond-shaped grey eyes.

"I'm so glad you're here." She picks up my bag, holds the door open and just like that I'm inside. I can't believe my luck. Another small miracle. Like I said before, love is a gamble. I think it's worth the risk, though.

The Least She Could Do

WHEN I PULL UP, MY MOTHER LOOKS out the front window of her half-duplex, smokes, waits for me, still wrapped in her blue bathrobe. I've taken her shopping every Sunday morning for years and every time I come over here I can't help comparing it to Dad's place. I defend Mom to everyone, even though I don't pretend to understand her myself. My brothers, Will Jr. and James, are still bitter, still complain that Mom should never have left Dad even though we had all moved out by the time they split. Dad refuses to talk about it; Mom just said it was long overdue.

Thinking about it now, I can see that there wasn't much affection between them, hadn't been for years. Not that they fought or anything like that, at least not in front of us. But there was a coldness, a formality between them that was always there as far as I knew. When you grow up in that kind of atmosphere, when that's all you know, it seems normal. One night when I was about twelve I had dinner at a friend's house and her parents acted so strange, I thought. They kidded with each other, they laughed. I even saw her father put his arms around her mother in the kitchen afterwards when they thought no one was looking. Until then I had no idea that married people could act like that.

～

On the drive home from my doctor's office his voice echoed, "Eudora, I'm afraid it's herpes."

Will wouldn't be home for hours so I had time to think about what I would say and do once the rage subsided. I'd been suspicious before, confronted him, and of course he denied it, tried to make me feel guilty for the accusation. A few months later he bought me a Mercedes for my birthday and I knew something was up. He pouted, disappointed that I didn't trust him. If it had happened earlier, in the first flush of our love, I would have called him on it right then and there, rushed down to his office in a torrent of tears, made a horrific scene. But now there were the kids to think about — Will Jr. was ten, James was nine, and Molly was six. I had no skills, no job, nowhere to go. I'd been his faithful and devoted companion for almost fifteen years. Would I take my children and live on alimony while he did what he pleased? Not on your life. Not before I was good and ready.

I pretended nothing was wrong, but I wasn't about to let it get messy. He could cheat on me, he could make me stop loving him, but he couldn't ruin the children's lives too. I would wait to make my move.

～

Dad remarried not long after the divorce. Roxanne was the blonde, athletic-looking daughter of one of his clients, who was now his father-in-law. He didn't talk about Mom or live with her, but aside from his "upgrade" replacement, Dad's life seemed unchanged.

Meanwhile, Mom had left our beautiful home in a prestigious neighbourhood, with a staff of five, to live alone in a half-duplex on a busy street. At first she seemed happy about the whole thing, said she'd never lived on her own before, and looked forward to her independence and freedom. She'd gone from my grandfather's highly regimented house to my father's, as many women of her age had, so I tried to be supportive. A year later, though, Mom slipped into a depression and withdrew from everyone, barely left the house except when I took her to the mall.

∽

I decided, after long and sober consideration, that the wisest thing to do was to play the dumb, happy housewife, do all the wifely things expected of a woman in my position: go to functions on his arm, entertain clients, hold teas for the social club's charity committee. Not that I didn't think it was all a load of horseshit from the word go. I always had. So I summoned all my dramatic abilities (I had wanted to study drama in university but my father had pointed to my nose and laughed) and put on the show of a lifetime. After all, no one knew about Matt and he was the one person who knew all about Will.

There was always a great attraction between Matt and me, and always something to get in the way of our acting on it. We'd known each other since high school and even then, when we met, we were both seeing other people. We both married soon after that. Over the years we'd see each other now and again at social affairs and there was usually the moment or so of eye contact over a drink, the helping in or out of a seat, the lingering embrace of a dance over too soon that made me certain it was still always there. The New Year's Eve after my doctor's prognosis we met again at the Club. Will had left early, swore to sue the kitchen for food poisoning. He'd be all right, he insisted, just needed to go home and sleep it off, and why didn't I just stay and enjoy myself? He was in such a rush to get to her he didn't notice I made no objections, made no attempt to go with him. I didn't, in fact, give a damn.

Before long, Matt made his way over to me. Helene had slipped on an icy patch in front of their house on Vale Avenue and sprained her ankle a few days before, but still gamely made it to the party on crutches. Dancing was out of the question. Over the course of the evening I told him about Will's unfaithfulness. He gave me a brotherly squeeze and told me I didn't deserve to be treated that way. He then went back to Helene, left me with a lump in my throat from saying too much. He caught me as I hailed a cab and gave me another squeeze, this one not so brotherly. "Happy New Year, Eudora. I'll be in touch," he whispered.

Matt called a few days into the New Year and we arranged to meet for lunch. Much as I wanted Matt, I couldn't let myself sink to Will's level, jeopardize my relationship with the children, and lose leverage in a divorce settlement. When I told him all this he promised friendship and loyalty. Which of course made me fall in love with him even more.

When Molly finally went to college nine years later, I was free to move out of Will's house, buy the half-duplex with the little bit of my own money I had, and be my own woman. Those early days here with Matt were some of the happiest of my life.

Molly tries to defend me in front of the boys and is fiercely loyal, but she's got it all wrong. She's convinced I'm a frail old lady, half-demented, who needs help to go the grocery store. The truth is, the poor girl has little more in her life than that job of hers. Many times I've nearly told her the truth, but I don't think she could handle it.

༄

One October afternoon, Helene called. As she spoke, I focused on the orange leaves of the mountain ash in my front yard against the flat grey sky. At first I was afraid she was calling to tell me that the jig was up, she'd found out about Matt and me. But instead she told me about Matt's stroke. She said she was sure that I would want to know, that he'd been in hospital since the night before. She gave me the room number.

By the time I got to the hospital, he was already gone. I saw the door to his room was closed and didn't want to barge in, so I checked in at the desk and they told me. Snow began to fall as I walked to my car, big, wet flakes that got in my eyes. I didn't cry, I didn't until later that night, amazed by Helene's grace. For she must have known.

I know there's no use in regrets. I try not to look back, but it's pretty hard not to. I should have left Will earlier; Matt and I would have had more time together. Instead I waited for the kids' sake, and now I wonder how much difference my waiting made to them. None, I think. Did the stress of our relationship contribute to Matt's stroke? Hard things to think about. And yet I don't seem able to stop myself.

∾

Roxanne and Dad seemed happy at first, happy like I'd never seen him and Mom. Roxanne loved to talk and make jokes, she was a real breath of fresh air. But she seems changed the last few times I've seen them. Quieter, withdrawn almost. Like something's bothering her. They had us kids over for dinner one night last fall and I don't think they actually looked at each other the whole time, let alone talk to each other. Roxanne was still very pleasant to us, but there was definite tension in the air between them. Will Jr. and James didn't say much, left as early as they possibly could.

Looking back, I guess we didn't talk much as a family. Certainly not about personal things. Sometimes I think we're little more than a group of strangers with the same DNA, given the cryptic nature of our family conversations. A few weeks ago we were on our way to Mom's doctor's new office and drove by the old Club, then down Vale Avenue. I said I hadn't been that way in a while.

"No," she said. "Not since the funeral."

"Funeral?"

"Matt Duncan's funeral. He died a few years ago."

The name didn't register with me. "Should I know him?"

"Just a friend of the family."

I have no idea what she was on about.

Now it's fallen to me to look after her, and I don't think she has any idea how busy I am, how much more complicated things are now from the way they were in her day. Then, you got married, you had kids. If you were lucky, like Mom was, you were rich and you had help. Now, it's a whole different thing. There's university, then there's a career. She wouldn't even want to think about what dating is like in this day and age. I'm sure it just would not compute with her, you know? Marriage, well, that's later if it even happens, and if it does, the two kids will hopefully show up sometime before you hit forty. So here I am, single and not loving it. Am I dating? No. I spend all my time ferrying her around, doing her lawn in the summers and the walks in winter. You'd think those rotten brothers of mine would pitch in with the yardwork, anyway. Don't get me wrong, I love her, but why the hell didn't she stay put? The way I look at it, she can't exactly go back to Dad after the way she hurt him, and then there's the little matter of Roxanne. I guess she's pretty much stuck, really, the way I'm stuck doing things for her. I suppose we'll both just have to make the best of it. Maybe I can convince her to sell the place and move into a condo, so I don't have to do the yardwork. It's the least she could do for me.

You Ain't Goin' Nowhere

WALKING IN ERLTON LAST NIGHT, I DIDN'T realize at first that I was on the street where Liz's house used to be. But I smelled leaves burning and immediately thought of the night of the fire. Then I looked at a sign and sure enough, this was the street. Of course, Erlton's no longer the wrong side of the tracks. It's all luxury condos now, looks like a different planet. They've left some of the bigger trees standing, though. I think I even found the huge elm with the scorch mark on one side that stood in her yard. Though it was hard to tell in the dark.

Then I thought of Mark. Sometimes people don't believe me when I tell them I used to sing in a folk duo with Mark Davidson from The Last Round-Up, the Juno award-winning country-rock band beloved of Canadians of a certain age. It was a long time ago, and it's not like The Last Round-Up was his only band. In fact The ???, the Edmonton punk outfit he'd just left before we started to sing together was his third band already. And he was only about twenty-one, like I was. We met when my band Speed Queen opened for The ??? during their week-long engagement at the Calgarian Hotel a couple of years earlier, in 1981. Mark's always been in a band, as far as I know. He's one of these people you just knew would make it. So, in the early nineties, when The Last Round-Up emerged with all those AM radio hits like "We Get on Like a House on Fire" and "Phoenix", I wasn't surprised. I only wondered, a little, what took him so long.

∞

Funny how everything seems to happen all at once, or not happen all at once. Within a couple of months, Mark left The ??? and I left Speed Queen. We both lost our part-time jobs — welcome to the recession — and we were both just out of long-term romantic relationships. He lived in the big old house across from the Stampede grounds that my friend Elizabeth rented. I could never keep track of who lived there at any given time. The House had become kind of a pit stop for bands on tour. People came and went and Mark had crashed on a couch in the basement for a while. I went over there to pick Liz up one Saturday night.

"Hey, Tina. Long time no see," he said as he changed the strings on his old Fender semi-acoustic. "You know, I've been thinking about you lately."

"Really? Why?"

"Would you want to form a folk duo with me?"

"A folk duo?" That was about the last thing I ever expected anybody to ask me. I mean, I knew Mark had a wide range of musical tastes. I did, too. I just never thought about a folk duo, especially not one with me in it.

"Sure. You and me, acoustic guitar and vocals. I'm writing some stuff right now. We could do some covers — Bob Dylan, of course. The Byrds, Johnny Cash."

"What about Hank Williams?" I asked. "And Gram Parsons?"

I really just asked him about Gram Parsons to bug him. I knew any folk-rockey kind of project of his would involve Gram Parsons covers. Mark loved Gram Parsons. He wanted to *be* Gram Parsons, the genius behind The Flying Burrito Brothers who'd died of an overdose in 1973 at age twenty-six. Mark was growing his dark, middle-parted hair out and he was even starting to look like Gram Parsons. It was a little freaky, I thought. And now did he think I'd be Emmy Lou Harris for him?

"Well, yeah. Hank, Gram Parsons, obviously," he answered. "So what do you think?"

I shrugged. I couldn't think of any reason not to. "Sure. Why not?"

"That's cool. I think we'd be good together. So you want to practice tomorrow?"

"In the afternoon. There's supposed to be five bands at The National tonight. Why don't you come with us?"

"I'm not into that shit anymore. It's all hardcore now."

"Yeah, I know. I'm not into it, either."

"So why go? Stay here and we'll get busy."

I laughed. "Hang on. We just started to talk about this. I'm going more to hang out with people than for the bands."

Liz fixed her blue rhinestone earrings as she came down the stairs. "You should try it sometime, Mark. You know, socializing."

You Ain't Goin' Nowhere

"Hey, I just went out and bought these strings today. And people troop through this house day and night. I don't have to go out to see them."

"Fine," she said. "Suit yourself, be a hermit. We're going out."

But as Liz and I sat in the smoke-filled National and drank our glasses of flat, sour draft and listened to the predictable, three-chord trash numbers with unintelligible lyrics (unintelligible except for "fuck off"), I started to wish I'd stayed back with Mark. He took things seriously, I thought. He was an artist, hard at work on a Saturday night while I listened to music I didn't even like because — I didn't even know why. Because I had nothing else to do. Because Jeff had left town, and he never called or wrote.

I decided to go home early so I'd be ready for practice the next day.

∽

On the bus on the way over to the House I'd wondered if this was a mistake, if Mark had been kidding. But he waited for me when I walked up to the front door.

"Hey, Tina. Glad you're here. I've got some songs ready to go."

I barely had time to take off my jacket before he handed me a sheet with the chords to The Flying Burritos' "Sin City" on it. And a plastic tumbler full of white wine. We were off.

∽

After a while, some people got this idea that Mark and I were lovers, or at least that he was in love with me. I never thought so. It was true, every night we played The Calgarian with The ???, he dedicated their version of "For Your Love" to me. It didn't mean anything — he just knew I dug The Yardbirds. He wasn't really my type — he was too short, too baby-faced. And I don't think I was his type, either. The girls I'd seen him with were dark-haired, pixie-ish, less curvaceous than me.

Mark seemed to me to be all business — well, all music, I mean. After a while though, I realized the cheap white wine he bought by the box flowed pretty freely during our practices — maybe he wasn't so serious.

One day, we finally nailed the harmonies in our Byrdsesque cover of Dylan's "You Ain't Goin' Nowhere". It was exhausting, singing the same line probably seventy-five times over, fingers stuck in our ears, trying to wind one voice around the other just the way Mark imagined it. I began to think he was crazy, that we'd never do what he wanted — when we suddenly did it. Whether he was a fraction of a tone down from before or I was a fraction of a tone up, or both, I don't know, but it sounded better than it ever had before. We did it again a few more times just to make sure we really had it, and then I had to sit down and light a cigarette.

"Oh, man. That was killer. You're a slave driver, Mark."

"Yeah," he said, and filled our glasses. "But it worked, didn't it?"

"Sure, it sounded great. I just don't know if we'll ever be able to do it again."

"Don't worry. We've got it down."

The first few weeks Mark had been very strict about keeping our practices to a minimum of two hours. But after a while they started to get shorter and our drinking wine and

You Ain't Goin' Nowhere

bullshitting time seemed to get longer. That day we worked very hard for an hour and that was it.

After Mark had a few drinks I noticed he started to talk more like a country singer, the same way some British people's accents sometimes seem thicker when they drink. "We ought to get ourselves a couple of them Nudie suits. You know, after we start to make some money."

"I like the one Hank Williams had with the staffs and notes down the sleeves and legs."

"That was pretty cool. But I liked Gram Parsons' better — ever seen pictures of it? It had marijuana leaves and poppies all over it."

I knew Gram Parsons would come up sooner or later. "Sounds cool. You need to get one." He'd be doing well if he could find the money for any suit, I thought. A suit at the Sally Ann, even, never mind a custom-made suit by Nudie, tailor to the stars. But he had to dream, didn't he?

He poured more wine. "Hey, did you ever read about Gram's funeral — well, his cremation?"

"Um, no. I didn't."

"See, he died in a hotel room in Joshua Tree, in California. His family wanted to bring his body back to Louisiana, but he'd wanted to be cremated at Joshua Tree. So his friends got some bogus paperwork and fooled the morgue into giving them the body. They took it out into the desert and lit it on fire. Unfortunately the police showed up and put the fire out and he ended up being buried in Louisiana after all. But isn't that a cool story?"

"It's crazy."

"What a way to go. That's got to be the coolest funeral ever. Someday I want to go to the Joshua Tree Inn, rent out Room 8. Soak up the vibes."

Seemed to me he'd already soaked up enough Gram Parsons vibes as it was.

∽

Liz started to get after me to date again soon after Jeff left town. I didn't want to, but she figured it was time. She was probably right. At a party one night, she introduced me to Keith, who sang in a band called The Serum. We started to talk and he seemed like a nice guy. He was also tall, and had clear grey eyes. After a while he asked if I wanted to go out for drinks sometime. I hesitated for a second. Was I ready for that? I started to dream up excuses not to when I noticed Liz looking at me from across the room.

"Yeah, all right," I said. "When is good for you?"

"What about Saturday night?"

"Sure. I'm practicing here until about 8:30, though."

"I could come and pick you up."

"Okay."

Maybe now Liz would get off my back.

∽

Mark and I practiced the day after I went out with Keith, got right to work on the Dylan song "Boots of Spanish Leather". It's a duet — of course, Dylan doesn't sing it that way, but he wrote it as one — so it worked really well for us. But Mark acted weird. Every time he sang the line, "Oh, but I just thought you might want something fine / Made of silver or of golden," he looked at me funny. I almost stopped to ask him, "What?", but I bit my tongue. Because there was this unspoken thing between us — we didn't talk about anything personal. We talked about music, yes. And we talked bullshit, but personal things seemed out of bounds.

After about an hour I went upstairs to go to the bathroom, and when I came back he'd rolled us a couple of cigarettes (tailor-mades cost too much) and filled our tumblers.

"Who was that guy who came to pick you up last night?" he asked as he looked out the window at the traffic.

I lit my rollie. "His name is Keith. Sings in a band called The Serum. You've probably heard of them."

"I think I have. He looks just like Jeff. You know that, don't you?"

"I guess he does. I didn't really notice," I said. *What the fuck, Mark? I thought. What is this? It's none of your goddamn business what I do, or who I do it with, or who they look like.*

After I finished my wine, I left. I told Mark I was tired, been out late. He said that was okay, he'd see me later. Only he didn't see me later, not for a while.

I skipped practices for a week, said I was sick. I'm sure he knew I was lying, but he didn't push it. He probably thought I was with Keith. Nothing could be further from the truth — after Mark pointed out Keith's resemblance to Jeff, I lost interest. Maybe I wasn't that interested in the first place. The next week I dropped by the house to see Liz and Mark answered the door.

"Hey, Tina. Feeling better?" he asked.

"Uh, yeah. Thanks."

"You didn't bring your guitar."

"No. I just came by to see if Liz was here."

He rubbed his stubbly chin for a minute before he answered me. Giving me a hard look in the eye, he said, "Sorry. She's not here right now. Listen, I was in the middle of something, but if you want to wait for her she should be back soon," he said and went back downstairs. I decided to leave, give Liz a call later.

After that I was depressed for a while, felt like I had nothing going on in my life at all. But when I started to think about it, things weren't so bad. Maybe I didn't have a job. Maybe I didn't have a love life, and maybe I still thought about Jeff way too much. But I sang in a folk duo. A pretty cool folk duo, too. And maybe Mark cared about me more than I realized — he must have, to say what he did. So one evening I decided to go and see how he was. He was probably dying for us to get back to work.

When I got off the bus I noticed a strong smell of smoke in the air, but didn't really think much about it. Until I got closer to the House and noticed the fire trucks that blocked the street in front of it. I couldn't help screaming when I saw the thick clouds of black smoke billow out the open front door. Was anyone inside? Liz, Mark? The firefighters wouldn't let me near the house and I felt like I'd go insane. I thought of Gram Parsons, wondered if Mark hadn't tried to conduct some kind of suicidal drunken tribute to his hero. Gram and Emmy Lou singing "We'll Sweep Out the Ashes in the Morning" stuck in my head. I paced the front lawn, felt like my crazily pounding heart would come exploding out my mouth.

It seemed like hours to me, but it was probably only a few minutes later that two firefighters helped Mark out. He

You Ain't Goin' Nowhere

coughed pretty hard, face full of black soot, but he seemed okay. He was alive, anyway, which was a relief.

"Where's Liz?" I asked him.

"Went to a movie. I was alone. You got a cigarette?" He was shaking pretty hard, looked around with the uncomprehending eyes of someone who's just been torn from sleep.

"Yeah, here. So what happened?"

He lit the cigarette and coughed some more. "I don't know," he finally said when he caught his breath. "One minute I'm sitting and listening to some tunes, and the next thing I know some firemen are dragging me out the door. Jesus Christ."

After the firemen left we started to clean up. The only thing that had actually caught fire was the old arm chair Mark had fallen asleep in with a lit cigarette in his hand. Its charred remains now sat, soaked, on the front lawn. But the smoke smell inside was awful, so we opened the windows. We found a bucket and a mop and washed the living room floor and walls. Liz was going to be furious with Mark, I knew, so cleaning up was the least we could do.

Mark insisted I stay and have a drink with him after we finished. I knew he'd drink whether I stayed or not, so I decided I might as well stay and keep an eye on him for a while. He was getting pretty maudlin.

"When I saw the fire trucks I was really worried about you, you know. I thought you might have been pulling some kind of Gram Parsons thing."

"Right. Listen, don't talk about him and me in the same sentence again. He was supremely talented. I am nothing compared to him. And I almost burned Liz's damn house down."

"You're not nothing."

"I got nothing happening in my life."

"You've got me. What about practising again sometime?"

"You mean it?"

"Sure. How about Tuesday?"

Maybe I imagined it, but I thought the idea of us practising again cheered him up. He seemed to look forward to it. So I was surprised when I showed up on Tuesday and found Mark in the living room, surrounded by his stuff. He sat on the remaining chair and rolled a cigarette. At his feet were a knapsack, his guitar and two plastic milk crates full of records. I could see what was going on, but for a minute I didn't comprehend.

"What's this?" I asked, and put my guitar down.

"Well, you probably know Liz is a little unhappy with me. So I'm catching a ride with Microcrystalline Cellulose. They have a gig in Seattle and then they go back to San Francisco."

"What is it with San Francisco? Everybody goes there."

"Aw, c'mon. You know why. They've had a great scene since the sixties. And you know there's nothing going on here. So I have to go."

I don't know if it was the suddenness, or maybe I was just tired of people leaving. Whatever it was I couldn't help crying a little. I think it surprised me more than him.

"I'm sorry," I said, and looked for a Kleenex in my purse. "I don't know what's wrong with me. I'm sure you'll have a great time."

He sat beside me and put his arm around me, kind of stiff-like, the way your uncle or your teacher might. "Go ahead and cry, Grievous Angel," he said, almost in a whisper. "I know you feel bad, and you have for a long time. Me, too, and that's another good reason for me to leave. See, you get this idea that life's supposed to be a certain way, or that a certain thing is supposed to happen. But it ain't like that. Life happens the way it happens, and you can't let it frustrate you. You can't let it eat away at you. So cry and then let it go. Life's got a lot to offer you."

He poured us each a small glass of wine, the end of his last box. "Besides," he said. "I want you to have my records."

He must have started drinking quite a bit earlier, I thought. "Your records? You can't be serious."

"Well, not the Gram Parsons ones. But the rest of them, yes."

"I couldn't do that, Mark. And I have lots of them already."

"What about the Dylan records? I want you to have them."

"I do have most of those."

"Okay, *Blood on the Tracks*. I know you don't have that one. I want you to have it."

I had to laugh a little. I hated that album. "Sure. Thanks. I'll think of you every time I listen to it."

We heard a horn outside, saw Microcrystalline Cellulose's dirty harvest gold Chevy van on the street. "I gotta run, Tina. You take care of yourself, Okay?"

"Sure, Mark. You, too. We'll see you sometime."

I watched him get into the van, watched it pull away. For a while I stood there and looked out the window. The room seemed very quiet with just me in it. Me and my guitar and *Blood on the Tracks*.

I never did see Mark again, not in person, anyway. But of course I've heard The Last Round-Up a million times on the radio. I have their albums. I've seen their videos. I think I even heard them on the canned music in my dentist's office last month, but it was hard to tell over the drill. Sometimes I wonder about their huge song from the mid-nineties, "Tangled Up in My Imagination", the one they always play at NHL games. The line where he sings, "Grievous Angel, don't you cry / Listen to my lullaby" — sometimes I wonder if he meant me. Of course knowing him, he probably meant Gram Parsons.

The Pass

WHENEVER MARIO TAKES A BATH HIS SLOW, solemn singing comes through the wall between our bathrooms, always the same song. "Old Macdonald . . . had a farm," he intones. "E, I . . . E, I . . . OOOOO."

    Mike laughs at Mario's singing. Usually I don't mind it, but now I have to watch out my front window instead of listening for Mike. I shouldn't, but I can't focus on anything else. I rush around, move magazines from one end table to the other, wipe the counter again and again. You'd never know we've been together six years.

    Mario stops singing, and soon I hear Mike's feet on the front step.

∽

Frank is another little coal mining town in the Crowsnest Pass a few minutes down Highway 3 from Blairmore, where I've lived for ten years. A hundred years ago, a chunk of Turtle Mountain slid off in the middle of the night and killed seventy people. Maybe the natives knew something. They called Turtle

Mountain "The Mountain That Moves". Mike says he doesn't even notice the slide site anymore, but when I see those boulders on both sides of the highway, both sides of the train tracks, some of them three times bigger than my car, I worry it'll happen again. Maybe it'll be Crowsnest Mountain next time, which I can see from the motel.

Mike says I just think too much.

༄

A lot of our guests at the Bluebird Motel are truckers like Mike, looking for a cheap place to crash. Sleep, I mean. That's how we met: I was cleaning his room and I left the door open for some air. Then in the mirror over the bathroom sink I saw a tall, dark-haired man behind me. For a second I was afraid, but then I smiled back at him.

"Are you Joyce?"

"Yes."

"The lady in the office said you might have found my watch."

It was under a chair. He was back the next week, came looking for me again.

༄

My family's farm is near Pincher Creek so sometimes I bring Mike with me for dinner. My parents seem to like him. Every time she calls, Mom asks when we're getting married. "When we save up some money," I'll say, or "When Mike gets a better job," but really we've never talked about marriage. I'd like to have him around all the time, but his job is on the road and that won't change when we're married. I guess it'll happen when it happens.

∽

Mike took me to the Frank Slide Interpretive Centre once. I didn't want to go. "You're afraid of it," he said.
"I'm not afraid. I think it'll be depressing."
"It'll be educational. Are you afraid of learning something?"
It seemed weird to look down at the silent mounds of rock that crushed all those people from the comfortable, air-conditioned viewing area. I mean, the local history was interesting. But I felt so sad. Nobody else looked sad: not the bored, noisy kids, not the elderly tourists complaining about the weather. I couldn't understand it. Mike read every display, but after a while it overwhelmed me. I kept thinking: all that happened in a few seconds and they had no idea. That's what terrifies me; something like that can happen with no warning.
"This is awful," I said. "It's so sad."
"But it happened a hundred years ago. It won't happen again. There are sensors and stuff on the mountain, now. We're safe."
But I didn't mean I was afraid. Suddenly I was irritable and tired. "I'm going to get a drink." He didn't answer, just kept reading.
I found a bench and drank my pop, tried not to look outside. How could I explain how I felt? But then, maybe you either get that kind of thing or you don't.

∽

Mario's resident manager of our building. He's also my friend, but he'd be a better friend if he wasn't such a pest. Sometimes he just starts. Like one morning, I was on my way out and he was cutting the grass.

"Going fishing with Mike again?"

"Yeah. It's a nice morning."

"So when are you two getting married?" he asks. Like we should be doing this right now instead of going fishing.

"Sometime, I guess."

He shook his head. "You think things will last forever. Anna died seventeen years ago. Sometime I think you better make the most of the time you got."

"Sure. That's a good point." I just didn't want to discuss it right then.

∽

We had no luck fishing on a cloudy Sunday morning. We packed up in silence, picked our way between the rocks along the bank of the Crowsnest River.

"I got a job in Thunder Bay," he said after a while. "In my brother's garage."

He'd grumbled about his job, but I didn't know he'd been looking for another. "When do you start?"

"Beginning of next month. I wanted to give some notice. It'd be rude just to up and quit."

Thunder Bay's a long way off. I've never been further east than Medicine Hat, never been much of anywhere. "I guess I could probably find something out there, too," I said.

"Well. That's the thing. I'm going by myself."

"Oh." I wanted to think of something else to say, something better. But I couldn't.

"See, my wife and I don't get along that well. But, still, she wouldn't understand. You know."

"How long have you been divorced?"

"We're not."

"But when ... "

"I'm in Thunder Bay part of the time."

He never mentioned Ontario. He was away for weeks sometimes, but said he was in BC or Saskatchewan. That would explain all the holidays he worked. He said it was because all the other guys were married. The last six years came tumbling out from under me; first one rock, then another, then a whole landslide.

I sat down on a boulder. He kept talking, but I couldn't hear him anymore. Part of me wanted to reach for him, try to keep him, but another part wanted to reach into his neck and rip out the veins. Meanwhile, he scrambled up the bank, onto the bridge and out of sight. He didn't look back once.

∞

I pack my stuff in my car, what didn't go at the yard sale. It was mostly Mario, spreading the word, dealing with the garage salers.

He gives me a brief, stiff hug. "I'll miss you. My brother used to live in Thunder Bay. He's dead now, otherwise I'd tell you to look him up."

I can't help laughing. Mario is bizarre sometimes.

"And I hope all the best for you and Mike."

NOTHING SACRED

He waves until he's just a little speck in my rear-view mirror. It was hard enough to tell my mom about Mike. I couldn't tell him, too. I wanted to, but lying was easier. I didn't even have to lie much; Mario made assumptions and I agreed.

My sister says there are lots of jobs in Lethbridge. Maybe I can find something besides motel work. I head east on the Number 3, through Frank, past the slide site. Somehow it doesn't seem as bad as before. Lethbridge is a lot farther away from the Pass, so I probably won't see Frank much again. Now it's behind me and I can hardly see it in the mirror anymore.

It looks so small.

Across the Universe

Walsh Junction, AB
Monday, December 5, 2005, 1:35 PM

"WILL YOU HAVE A BIG FAMILY DINNER when you get to New York?" the woman in the seat next to me asks.

"Oh, probably not until my brother gets home, too. He won't be back from Europe until the twenty-second. He's been over there researching a film he's making."

"Oh, my, that's exciting, isn't it?"

"Isn't it?"

I hope she gets off the bus soon. She keeps falling asleep and leaning on me and she smells like she could use a bath. It's actually better than when she's awake making chit chat, asking me questions. I make up any old answer I want, like the filmmaker brother I don't have.

The sun is bright as we pull out of this town near the Alberta-Saskatchewan border. There's lots of snow out this way, now it feels a little more like December. We haven't had any snow in Calgary yet this year; it's one of those dry, brown southern Alberta winters, bad for grass fires. I've been on this bus since eight-thirty this morning and it's almost two-and-a-half days until I get to New York. I've taken the Greyhound from Calgary to Vancouver before, even rode it out to Victoria once. That'll seem like nothing compared to this trip. It's almost three thousand miles.

∞

When it happened that Monday night in 1980, I was working in Jeunesse, formerly the Misses' Wear department at the downtown Bay. We'd just started to open Monday and Tuesday nights for Christmas shoppers, and it was dead, dead, dead. I finished my homework by 6:30. Could have shot off a cannon and not hit any one, said Peg over in Career Wear. Pretty much the only customer was an old transvestite who wanted to try on angora sweaters. I wasn't supposed to let him into the ladies' change rooms, but I didn't care. There weren't any managers around. I hoped he'd come out and show me how they looked, but he didn't. Later, I took an extra-long break in the cafeteria. It seemed that night would never end.

Finally I got home and flipped through my records, tried to decide what to listen to. I was so brain-dead from my shift, I couldn't think. Then my friend Kevin called.

"Hey, Kev. What's up?"
"Are you by a radio?"
"Yeah. Why, is your band on CJSW again?"
"No, Maggie. It's so weird. John Lennon's been shot."
"Get out of here. Who would shoot him?"
"I'm not kidding. Turn it on to CBC."

Across the Universe

I sighed, switched on the radio and tuned it to CBC, expected to hear a Neil Young song, or something even worse. Kevin was quite a prankster. But this time he wasn't joking. John Lennon had been shot outside his New York apartment building, the announcer said. He'd been rushed to hospital, but they couldn't save him.

Moosomin, SK
Tuesday, December 6, 2005, 12:50 AM

More snow as we moved through Saskatchewan in the afternoon and evening. I always forget how flat it is, too. The white and grey prairie seemed to roll out in front of us forever, while there was still enough light to see it. We're stopped in this little town near the Manitoba border for a bathroom/smoke break. Lots of the other passengers are sleeping, but I can't, never sleep well when I'm travelling.

The last song I listened to on my iPod was "Tomorrow Never Knows", from the *Revolver* album. I don't listen to Beatles albums much anymore; I skip all the Sir Paul songs as well as the George and Ringo songs, which I've skipped for many years. One day I'll get organized and burn all the John songs onto their own CDs. The thing is, it can still depress me, even now. I'll listen for a while, but then it gets to be too much. I got the *Lennon Legend* CD a few years ago, a greatest hits collection. It's hard to listen to, because it's in chronological order. There's the good stuff at the beginning, but then the sappy stuff from *Double Fantasy* starts. That album got mediocre reviews, and then he was killed and all of a sudden it was number one and practically every song off it became a single, and it was so sad. Sad because he was dead, sad because that last album was just so damn dull. And don't get me wrong, I loved him. But it was a dull album before he died; then it became a dull, depressing album.

But now the song is John Lennon's cover of "Stand By Me" from *Rock'n'Roll*, an album I can always listen to with pure pleasure. It's a collection of fifties standards he put together in 1975 with a fantastic group of musicians, produced by Phil Spector. It never occurred to me to get an iPod before Brian gave me this one for my birthday last year. He said I'd like it. I do like it, but it was part of his campaign to get me to stop listening to "old music". When he gave it to me, he'd already put a bunch of music on it, his music. I don't even know what a lot of it is. For a while I started to think he was right, that I should get with the times. That the stuff I listened to was bad, wrong somehow. Not cool. I started to listen to my stuff on the sly, when I was alone or on shift in the store. Then I realized I was embarrassed to like what I like, for a while. How stupid is that? So now I've taken his music off the iPod and replaced it with mine. Still, every time I look at it I think of him.

Portage La Prairie, MB
Tuesday, December 6, 2005, 4:20 AM

Can't see much outside besides the road in front of us and the falling snow in the bus' headlights. The bus is quiet except for rumbles of snoring from the aisles. I try to sleep and I do doze off momentarily sometimes, but it isn't really working. Now I'm starting to fret. I'm a middle-aged woman riding a bus three thousand miles to mourn a man I never met who died twenty-five years ago. I'm older now than he ever was. And nobody cares that I'm doing this. Not Brian, not my family.

Across the Universe

Not John Lennon, God knows. It's actually putting Crystal out, I forgot about that. This time tomorrow, I'll be in Central Park with all the other freaks and losers and weirdos, and we'll all sing "Give Peace a Chance" or "Imagine", sway back and forth holding candles, tears streaming down our faces. Part of me can't believe I'm doing this. I'm not one of those weird people who hang out at Graceland or outside the Dakota or make pilgrimages to Jim Morrison's grave. Yet here I am.

Crystal was pissed when I asked for a week off at the beginning of December, right in the middle of our busiest season. Especially when she found out why. "You're not really going to do that," she laughed.

"Why not?"

"It's stupid."

That helped me to make up my mind, actually. I've never been to New York before and I wanted to take two weeks, wanted to arrive early so I could look around, but Crystal made me feel guilty, so instead I'll get there at 5:30 in the morning on December 8th. Still, that should give me a little time to explore.

∾

Brian and I went to a movie one night last winter, a couple of weeks before Christmas. That night was cold, snowing little dry, hard flakes like ice crystals. He'd been quiet all night and didn't say much on the way home. He drove past my apartment building, down the street by the park. He pulled over, parked the car, turned and looked me in the eye.

While he spoke I looked at the frost-covered branch of an ash tree on the riverbank, lit by a streetlight. He said it wasn't working between us anymore, gave me all that stuff about it isn't you, it's me, let's still be friends and all that crap. Then he told me not to cry. If I'd been able to, I would have said, "After five years all you have is clichés? Don't you have the guts to tell me what's really going on? All I want is the truth. Just gimme some truth."

But all I could do was cry. Merry fucking Christmas, Brian.

Since then the worst part of it has been realizing how wrong I was about Brian. I thought we were on the same page, I thought we understood each other. Had I been going around for that entire five years with all these wrong ideas about him? Or had something suddenly changed? I guess I'll never know. I guess it doesn't matter, either, not now.

∽

The press called it an assassination, then they changed it to murder, like they thought calling it an assassination gave him too much gravity, too much importance. What was he but a self-taught musician, after all? And then all the theories about who did it and how and why started to pop up. The insane fan theory, of course. The US government-backed brainwashed assassin theory, masterminded by either Ronald Reagan or George Bush, Sr., depending on where you read it. The CIA did have a massive file on him. I've read a theory that Stephen King did it, based on the similarity in looks between him and Mark David Chapman, and given King's gory writings. There's even some nut out there with a web page saying Paul McCartney did it, claims it's a Mozart-Salieri kind of situation.

An interviewer once asked Lennon how he thought he would die. What a question. He said he thought some loony would probably pop him off. Am I a loony, am I getting into my own little Mark David Chapman space, here? Yet we all need heroes, don't we?

Dave, the old hippie who'd owned Records Galore, got a charge out of Crystal and me when we used to come into his store Saturdays when we were twelve or thirteen. The Beatle girls, he called us and after a while he started to save us stuff. Ten years ago Crystal got her dad to buy the store after his retirement and now she and I run the place. We've been Records Galore and More for five years now. We still sell records and CDs, books and memorabilia, but now we also carry incense, jewelry, posters, magazines, that kind of thing. I think we should branch out into coffee, but she says we could never compete with the Starbucks down the road. Maybe she's right.

I *will* be a loony if I don't get some real sleep sometime soon. I doze off for maybe a half-hour at a time, but that's all I can manage. Man, this is a long trip.

Kenora, ON
Tuesday, December 6, 2005, 10:15 AM

There's even more snow once we get into Ontario. The driver points out Lake of the Woods as we approach Kenora. One of the people who get on at this stop is a young girl, who sits beside me. She's blonde, about sixteen. I don't know, it's hard for me to tell anymore, maybe she's older. But she doesn't look old enough to be out of school. She's reading *The Catcher in the Rye*, the book Chapman was apparently reading at the time he killed John Lennon.

She's the age I was in 1980. I remember being in shock for weeks after it happened. I went to school the next day but I couldn't concentrate on anything. Crystal and I skipped classes that afternoon and went and hung around downtown, wandered aimlessly, as though that might help us to understand. We eventually ended up at Records Galore. Dave looked about the way we felt, just shook his big bearded head. He said he'd sold every Beatle-related item he had in the store before noon. The three of us stood and looked out the front window of the store a long time, watched people trudge by through the snow.

Since then, I'm always depressed at the beginning of December, which is why I can't believe Brian chose this time of year to break up with me. It was last December 11th, exactly two weeks before Christmas. I was just starting to feel better, starting to get into the holiday mood a bit, and then he goes and takes me down. Let me take you down. This year, I think people feel I should get over it, move on. Well, dammit, I guess I'll get over it when I'm ready. How long is it supposed to take? I mean, I was with him five years. I won't just get over him overnight. I heard he moved to Kelowna in the summer. He always complained about the city getting too big, too crowded, too much traffic. And I agreed with him. I wanted to leave too, together.

Highway 11 Between Raith, ON and Thunder Bay, ON
Tuesday, December 6 2005, 6:25 PM

I do have one song from *Double Fantasy* on my iPod. "Watching the Wheels" is playing and ironically, we're not moving. We've been pulled over at the side of the road in the middle of a blizzard for almost an hour. The wind screams around us and you can't see a thing. Something's wrong with the bus too, I think. The driver's been outside, around the back a fair bit, and on the radio a lot. He hasn't said much to us yet and people are getting nervous.

I knew something would happen. I've thought of doing this for twenty-four years and now that I finally get the chance, what happens?

The girl next to me finally looks up from her book.

"I wonder what's wrong," she says.

"I don't know. The driver said there was a mechanical problem. I just hope we can get going pretty soon."

"You on a tight schedule?"

"I have to be in New York tomorrow."

"I'm sure we'll get going pretty soon. Can't do much about the storm, though."

Thunder Bay, ON
Wednesday, December 7, 2005, 12:07 AM

We got moving eventually, crawled along the side of the highway and finally made it to the Thunder Bay bus depot. The storm still blasts and they say no buses will leave until it breaks. In the meantime, the depot is full of tired, pissed-off passengers. A group from my bus huddle in a corner and I overhear them complain.

"I'm demanding a refund."

"I can't believe there's not even a restaurant."

"Do they really expect us to drink coffee from a vending machine?"

I can't even go there. Because I can't believe it, my trip is just evaporating in front of my eyes. If we don't leave soon, I'll miss the whole thing. Even under ideal conditions, it's still supposed to be twenty-four hours until we get to Buffalo and then another ten to New York. Even if we left right now, I'd arrive in New York around 10:00 AM on December 8th not taking into account customs or the road conditions.

Sleep is the only thing that makes any sense right now. But I can't. There's nowhere to stretch out and you can't even slouch in these plastic seats. Besides, there's too much noise, and I'm too mad. Late again. It seems like I'm late for everything. Not little things like arriving on time, I'm always on time. But the big stuff — I'm always late for that. Too late for sixties music. Too late to get a real career. Too late to have a family. Here I am, sleep-deprived, sitting in a bus depot in Thunder Bay, too late for the twenty-fifth anniversary of John Lennon's death. I'll miss the whole thing. I'm so mad I can't even cry. I just sit here, grind my teeth. Brian, this is your fault. I wouldn't be in this stupid bus depot by myself in the middle of the night if you hadn't left me. I would be in our bed, asleep, with your arms around me. This shouldn't be happening to me. My life is a mess.

Fuck.

ᛰ

I must have been even more exhausted than I thought, because I managed to sleep for over five hours, the longest I've been able to this whole trip. And in this lousy chair, too. Outside the drifts of snow are three, four feet high, and there's very little traffic besides a few snowplows and police cars. Now it's

7:30 AM and the ticket office is open. Almost everybody in the place rushes the counter, wants a refund, an explanation, an apology, something. I don't see the point.

Catcher in the Rye girl comes and sits down beside me. "How come you're not up there complaining?" she asks.

"About what? The weather? What can they do about that?"

"I know. I mean, things happen sometimes and there's nothing you can do. You just have to let it go."

"Exactly."

"Did you say you had a meeting in New York?"

"Yeah. It looks like I'm going to miss it. I don't think it matters, though. What about you?"

"I'm on my way back to Toronto. Not in a big hurry."

"Good for you."

Bassano, AB
Thursday December 8, 2005, 4:30 PM

After some negotiation in the Thunder Bay bus depot, I managed to get them to cancel my fare to New York and give me a ticket home. We're back on the prairies now and they've had quite a bit of snow out here, too, since I left. I can see the sun again, even though it's on its way down, and I feel better. Lighter, though I don't know why that should be. Must be the iPod — I decided to give it to *Catcher in the Rye* girl. Dayna's her name. She was very grateful, although I'm sure she thinks I'm nuts. Whatever. She's not the first.

So it turns out I'll be in Calgary on December 8th, 2005 after all. I thought about going to the store, since that's where we ended up that awful day twenty-five years ago. But to hell with it. I'll be there enough over the next little while. In return for letting me go on this little pilgrimage, Crystal said I'd have to work our Boxing Week sale, so I'll be in every day from Boxing Day to New Year's Eve, absolutely our nuttiest week of the year. And here I thought I'd be spending the holidays alone.

Hamburg Blues

THIS IS A GOOD TIME TO HIT Javahead she thinks, and looks around. The lunch crowd is gone but the kids aren't out of school yet. Maybe noon isn't such a bad time to get up after all, in spite of the guilt trip her mother always gives her about it. She hangs her vintage faux-leopard coat on a hook, sits at a terminal and thanks the young woman who brings over her cappuccino plus. Plus Sambuca to ward off the cold.

Now she's ready to check her e-mail. First, though, she hits the William S. Burroughs website, but nothing is updated. Okay. E-mail time. Depressingly, only one new message. But it is from Stefan, a nurse who works the night shift in a psychiatric hospital in Hamburg. It's a stressful job, to say the least, and he surfs for relaxation. Andi met him a few months earlier in a poetry chat room; not that she writes a lot of poetry *per se*, but she does write song lyrics. And poets are interesting people, no question about that. "I'm glad to know a poet of Canada," he said in one of his early e-mails. "Does Canada have a tradition of poetry?" She smiles every time she thinks of it. Then again, before Stefan her idea of Germany was beer and oompah bands. Expressionist art, maybe. She probably said some funny things in her messages to him, too.

In today's missive, he's after her again to come visit him. "You'd love the canals, the beautiful old buildings. We have some great *kunsthallen* — art galleries. And I know you'd like to visit some of the bars and nightclubs in the Reeperbahn area, where The Beatles started out." That would be cool to see. Part of her would love to go to Germany. Or anywhere. *Hell, I could move there. What would it matter, what would it take me away from?* The band, of course.

The latest incarnation is called Cultureshocktherapy, to Stefan's amusement. Recently, she realized of all the members of her first band, Original Sin, she was the only one still at it. When they started out almost twenty-five years ago she never would have imagined it, but everybody else is married, has kids, boring jobs. Andi's been in some kind of band all along, couldn't think of quitting. She can hardly keep track of the young bassists and drummers who show up for a few practices, giggling girlfriends in tow, and then disappear.

Now Cultureshocktherapy plays clubs, community hall gigs, house parties like Original Sin did in the old days. Right back at the bottom, full circle. But that doesn't really matter. She doesn't expect, anymore, to become a rock star. Who ever heard of a 40-something emerging rock star? In fact, she's been thinking half-seriously of restyling the band as a blues act. You can play the blues into your eighties and beyond, it's not ageist the way pop music is. Pop's all about Avril Lavignes and Gobs, people who weren't even born when she started to work the bar circuit. All the same, she has to do it. So, she can't go to Hamburg; she's tried to explain this to Stefan before. She'll try again.

Dear Stefan:

Good to hear from you. I don't think I can make it to Hamburg. The band's important to me in a way that's hard to explain. The stage is the one place I can pout, pose, strut, wail, croon, be the brave and beautiful self of fantasy. Under the lights, black hair wild, face china white, lips ringed scarlet, I still look damn good. Don't get me wrong, I know I'm not twenty anymore. I don't have any illusions about being a star, but I have to keep doing it. In spite of the fact that some of our members have quit, like rats from a sinking ship (good band name).

There's another, more compelling reason for me to stay here. Money. It's very kind of you to offer to let me stay with you. I've always depended on the kindness of strangers. Not that you're really a stranger. I could ask Mom for the money and I'm sure, after a huge hassle, she'd give it to me, but she makes it clearer and clearer as the years go by that she doesn't appreciate subsidizing me. Ironically, money's been the only way she relates to me, the only way of relating she's ever known. Even so, I don't think money means much to her. I never meant much to her either; she was always traveling, sticking me into new schools. She bought me a condo out of guilt. I would rather not ask her for more unless it's absolutely necessary.

I'll speak frankly and admit something that I have never admitted to anybody. In fact, I'm only now becoming aware of it myself. The thing is, I hate change.

I hate difficulty. It sounds weird, but there you are. Until recently, I've thought of myself as something of an iconoclast, but it occurs to me lately that the rebellion in my life is superficial: my hair, the places I hang out at, my kooky clothes. Why am I still playing in garage bands into my 40s? Because I hate change. Not being in a band would be a big change. Why have my numerous relationships with men failed miserably? Because I hate difficulty. And relationships are difficult, they're hard work.

So I can't come to Hamburg because I hate change, I hate difficulty. And I'd hate to lose this, being able to open up to you like this. There's an ease in telling you all this, when I know you're halfway around the world. All that would change if we met.

I had a long pause, Stefan, after I wrote that last paragraph. I stood outside, lit up a Dunhill, watched people trudge through the snow, go in and out of the old sandstone library across the street. I'd like to come to Hamburg. I'd like to meet you, very much. But I'm afraid. If you can convince me, though, I'll come. I've been in this same city, listening to the same music, doing the same things, even smoking the same blasted cigarettes for a long time now. A change would be scary for someone like me, someone so strangely settled in her ways, as I now understand it. Tell me there's still hope for me. Tell me I'm not already becoming crotchety. Tell me again how you'd love to meet me.
Fond regards,
Andi

Hamburg Blues

She stops, mouse in hand, and considers a while. *I can't really send this to him. I can't expose myself like this. I don't know him, not really.* She clicks on Edit at the top of the screen, then Select All. She's about to hit backspace, delete the whole thing, start all over, tell him she can't come because the band is going into the studio. Then she swallows hard, hits Escape. The Edit window disappears and she clicks on Send. She waits a few seconds. "Mail sent".

She logs off, finishes her cappuccino, slips on her coat and steps outside. The cold wind bites her face, but she smiles, hardly notices. She lights up another Dunhill, wonders what the weather is like in Hamburg, what the music scene is like over there. Maybe there's a big demand for blues singers, you never know.

You Tore Me Down

FIONA WAITED A DISCREET LENGTH OF TIME after the mail carrier left. Discreet was when the carrier had got, say, two doors down the block from hers. She hated to look too eager for the mail to come, didn't want anyone to think she was just sitting and waiting for it to arrive. She opened the door, had to set one foot in the fresh snow to get to the mailbox. She riffled through the stack of bills, flyers addressed "To the lady of the house". Oh, and another rejection from a literary magazine she'd sent a story to four months ago. Damn good thing I've been dumped so many times, she reflected. Good preparation for being a writer. But maybe this wasn't a rejection; usually they send it to you in your own self-addressed stamped envelope, not the magazine's stationery. Who knows, she thought, and ripped the envelope open. Maybe I actually sold something.

Dear Fiona Baumgartner:
Thank you for submitting your short story entitled "You Tore Me Down" to The Castle Review. We wish to

suggest some changes, with an eye to possible publication in a future issue.

"YES!" she yelled, and thrust her fist in the air. "It's not a rejection . . . really." She continued reading.

We wondered if the main character, Porphyria, could be changed from a blonde to a redhead. Also, we felt the story might ring a little more true if it was set in Calgary instead of Vancouver. If you could make these changes and send it back to us, we will contact you promptly to let you know of our decision.

Sincerely,

The Editorial Collective

Fiona tried not walk, not run, to her computer. Strange changes to ask for. The character's hair colour? And the city? But, she reasoned, since she lived in Calgary and not Vancouver, they probably thought she'd be able to render it more faithfully. After all, no doubt the Editorial Collective knew what it was talking about. She'd change the main character to an Armenian sword swallower and the setting to Planetoid X-47 as long as they printed the damn story.

Two weeks later another letter arrived from *The Castle Review*. Fiona tore at the envelope as she watched the letter carrier trudge through the snow on the other side of the street. She read the letter a couple of times before she sat down, bewildered.

Dear Fiona Baumgartner:

Thank you for making the suggested changes to your short story, "You Tore Me Down". We feel the story is much improved and we are very interested in including it in a future issue of The Castle Review. *However, we would like to suggest the following additional changes:*

Make the male character, Bart, a little more sympathetic. We don't think he really could have meant to break Porphyria's heart. She probably just took what he said the wrong way. Girls are always doing this.

Mention Porphyria's bust size, specifying that it is ample. Additional detail about clothing she wears would also be welcome.

Clarify the date of the alleged dumping. January 1985 sounds about right.

After making these changes, please send it back to us and we will contact you as soon as possible. Thank you.

Cordially,

The Editorial Collective

Who the hell was this damned Editorial Collective anyway? Her hands shook as she searched the letter for a phone number. She grabbed the phone and began to dial, but hung up rather than act in haste. Later that afternoon, she did call, more curious than angry now.

"You've reached *The Castle Review*. No one is here to take your call right now . . . "

"Shit!" she hissed. She was about to hang up the phone when she heard someone interrupt the answering machine message, "Hello, hello?"

"Uh, yes. Hello. Am I speaking to one of the members of the Editorial Collective?" she asked.

"You are. In fact, I am the Editorial Collective. What can I do for you?"

You Tore Me Down

Fiona was sure the voice sounded familiar. "David!" she roared. "Is that you?"

After a short silence the voice asked, "Who is this?"

"This is Fiona Baumgartner! Are you David Laurier?"

"Well, yes. How are you, Fiona?"

"How am I? What is the meaning — I mean, what are you trying to do to me here, David?"

"Well, imagine how I felt when I read this story. I get your submission, see your name and I think, fine, we'll see what old Fiona's up to these days — "

"Old!" she interrupted.

"Take it easy, it's just a figure of speech. So I'm reading this story and here it's about the last time we saw each other."

"How was I supposed to know that *you'd* be reading it? I mean, what's with this 'Editorial Collective' shit?"

"It *was* an Editorial Collective until six months ago. I'm the only one left. I don't want to go into it right now."

"Fine with me. Anyway, after you read it, why didn't you just send me a rejection letter?"

"Because I want to run it. It's well-written."

"Okay. I'm glad you think so. But, c'mon, what's with all these changes?"

"I just wanted to make it more authentic."

"Authentic? David, it's not a documentary. It's a work of fiction."

"I beg to differ. I knew what was going on. I have to say, you've got a pretty good memory. But can you really call this a work of fiction?"

"I have a great memory when it comes to trauma. I can remember every gory detail. And, yes, it's a work of fiction.

I mean, it happens to be based on a true incident . . . and if anybody other than you had read it, it wouldn't matter. But it's my story, David, and I don't want to make those changes."

"Okay. I don't really want you to. Actually, I was just messing with your mind. I'll run it in the next issue."

She let out a sigh of relief. "As it ever was."

"What's that supposed to mean?" he asked.

"It means you haven't changed an iota. Messing with my mind, after all these years."

"What about you? You're like a . . . I don't know what. You haven't forgotten a single word I said to you, after all these years."

Fiona pulled together all the dignity she could find within. "Perhaps it was because I cared, David," she replied coolly.

"And I suppose you think I didn't!"

"It certainly seemed that way. But never mind. I don't want to have this discussion. I'm so *over* you, you know. I haven't thought about you in years. And I rescind my story. I withdraw it. Don't you dare run it!"

"You can't do that! It's a great story."

"You really think so?" she asked quietly.

"Sure. How could I not love it? C'mon, let me publish it. Just this once."

She thought for a moment. "Okay."

There was an awkward pause.

"So, other than writing, how are you doing?" he ventured.

"I'm okay. And you?"

"Oh, not so bad for an old guy. Listen, did you know we pay our contributors now?"

"No kidding. How much?"

You Tore Me Down

"Thirty dollars for a short story."

"Great. That should just about cover this call."

"Good, good. It was nice talking to you, Fiona."

"You, too, David."

"Feel free to send more stories, anytime."

"Sure. I will. Goodbye."

Fiona hung up the phone and looked out the front window, focused on the letter carrier's footprints in the snow on the steps. The walk needed clearing, she realized. She put on her boots and coat and found the shovel.

"Old!" The word came out as a frozen cloud as she threw the first shovelful onto the lawn.

The Poor Little Rich Girl

March 28, 1979

I ASKED THAT NEW GIRL TO OPEN the window so I could smell the cherry blossoms. I've always loved that smell — it reminds me of when Duber and I married. It would have been our fifty-ninth anniversary today. So what do you think she did? She opened the window. She didn't tell me I might get a chill, she didn't make a fuss, she just did what I asked. Maria, that's her name. I like her.

The rest of them think I'm insensible, that I'm so old, or so drugged up that I have no idea what goes on. Here's something none of them know, not even Buddy — I write in here every day. I keep this book under my mattress and when I say I don't want to be disturbed, they know I mean it. I didn't work my whole life so I could be treated like an invalid in my so-called golden years. Whatever goes on with my body, I still run this place, whether they want to believe it or not. Adolph Zukor said once that if I hadn't been an actress, I would have been the head of United States Steel. He didn't know the half of it.

The Poor Little Rich Girl

Buddy has the staff treat me like a child. Funny that I'd end up a child only in my eighties. I worked since age five, and my age never seemed to correspond with what I actually did in life, ever — I spent my childhood working, I spent my film career playing children. I made a fortune playing one child after another on the screen in my twenties and thirties. Now I'm treated like a child, something more delicate than a child. Buddy has them go through the newspapers before they bring them up to me with my lunch — breakfast, whatever it is — and clip out any articles that might upset me. Some days I want to tell them, look, leave my papers alone. Miss Pickford's a tough old gal. How do you think I got where I am, by pretending reality doesn't happen? But then, I guess I did get here by pretending, all right. And when I read about things like the Tate murders, I think maybe I don't need to keep up with reality. I feel like I'm a relic from a different world.

Where's Tony with my whiskey, anyway? He said he'd be right up.

⁓

There were six of us on staff at Pickfair: Tony was Miss Pickford's butler and Manuel was the driver — he took care of the garden, too, since Miss Pickford never went out and Mr. Rogers hardly ever did, either. Margaret was the nurse, Rita was the cook, Lupe cleaned and did the laundry. I covered for Rita and Lupe evenings and weekends. It was a long way on the bus from East L.A., but Mama was excited I had a job in Beverley Hills.

"You work for a movie star now, Maria," she said, in a hushed tone. As though I'd somehow made it now. A friend of Mama's got me the job. Before that I used to work at Taco Bell. I didn't mind it, but Mama didn't think they gave me enough hours. I think she just thought I spent too much time with Ramon.

"I think so," I said. "Her name is Mary Pickford."

"Never heard of her."

"They said she was in silent movies."

"Well, no wonder I never heard of her. How old do you think I am?"

Tony said there were eighteen on staff once, in the twenties when Miss Pickford and her ex-husband Mr. Fairbanks entertained. He said royalty and all kinds of famous writers and scientists, not just movie people, had dinner at Pickfair in those days. You'd never know it by 1979. The only people that ever came then were delivery people, doctors and sometimes Miss Pickford's stepson, Mr. Fairbanks, Jr. Even when he came, most of the time he didn't actually go up to her room. He came to see her and she talked to him on the intercom. Can you imagine?

Things like that kind of scared me at first. I used to wonder if the old lady wasn't dead already, if she wasn't a ghost. She was so skinny, almost a skeleton, and when she took that wig off, she just had little fine wisps of hair left, like an old man. Or a baby. I didn't understand why a rich movie star wouldn't get a better wig. The one she had was old and hideous. Tony said Miss Pickford was very frugal, she knew the worth of her money very well. Maybe she was frugal but she paid us well, and that's why I stayed. And I got used to her after a while. She seemed like a very sad old lady to me. I didn't want to think of ending up like that myself some day.

The Poor Little Rich Girl

～

April 1, 1979

Not long until my eighty-seventh birthday. I guess Doug Jr. will visit. Jayar, I call him. I'm not sure I want to see him. I wish people wouldn't make a fuss about my birthdays. Once you get as old as I am — eighty-five, ninety — what's the difference? Who cares anymore?

I look at the doll on the shelf across from my bed a lot lately, the one David Belasco bought me when I was on Broadway in The Warrens of Virginia. *I was fourteen, had already worked for nine years by then. When Jayar gave a party here a few years ago, Pearl Bailey, the singer, came up to my room. She said she'd dreamt about the doll, which was strange, since we'd never met before. She asked if she could take it to have its china head fixed. She said when the doll was mended, I'd be better, too.*

Pearl brought the doll back a month later and it looked wonderful, better than new. She said it took so long because they had to send away to Germany for a new head. I was touched, almost overcome with gratitude. We didn't mention what she'd said before about me mending, too, but I thought about it, and I'm sure she did. If only it were that easy. If only they could send away for a new head for me, replace and redistribute some of the old stuffing in my worn-out body. If I were really a doll, like the public imagined for so many years, a now-forgotten doll. But it just isn't that simple. I've always been practical, if nothing else, and I know it isn't that simple.

～

NOTHING SACRED

One day not long after I started at Pickfair, I took the sandwich Rita made me and walked around the halls on my lunch break, looked at all the photos and paintings of Miss Pickford. I wasn't really thinking about them, though. I was thinking about the argument Mama and I had about Ramon before I left for work. She never wanted me to see him in the first place. She didn't want me to see anyone — she thought I was too young. But I was eighteen, done high school. An adult, not much younger than Mama was when she got married. She thought Ramon was too handsome, too full of himself. She didn't trust him, or me.

"You just don't trust me," I'd said, "because of what happened to Carmela."

"You think you're smarter than your cousin? You think she's stupid enough to have a baby and you're not?"

"I didn't say Carmela was stupid. I only said you don't trust me."

"And I don't. You're too serious about Ramon. I want you to stop seeing him."

I didn't answer, slammed the door, walked to the bus stop. Mama always worried that I wasn't "being good". What did that even mean? She didn't want me to end up like Carmela was what she meant, pregnant and alone. Now, Mama, she was good. Though I couldn't see how things were that different for her than they were for my cousin. My father died when I was too little to really remember him, killed in an accident on the night shift at the meat packing plant where he worked. So Mama was alone, just like Carmela. I could never say that to her, though, because Mama had been married to my father. She was a good Catholic.

The Poor Little Rich Girl

Not like Carmela. Tia Adriana called one night and after a few minutes, Mama let out a groan, sounded like she was in pain. It scared me. I figured someone had died.

"What happened?" I asked when she hung up.

"Your cousin Carmela. She's pregnant. She's only seventeen. Wicked girl."

Tony came up behind me then, brought me back to my lunch break at Pickfair, nodded at the huge oil portrait I stood in front of. "That's Miss Pickford in one of her biggest films, *The Poor Little Rich Girl*," he said. "She made that picture in 1917. Over sixty years ago." Tony could tell you whatever you wanted to know about Miss Pickford.

"She sure was beautiful."

"She was very beautiful. She was the first real movie star, and the most powerful woman in Hollywood. You know, in 1917 she made $10,000 a week. Most men did well to make a few dollars a day then."

"That's amazing."

We walked further down the hall to some family photographs. "These must be Miss Pickford and Mr. Rogers' children, right?" I asked.

"Yes, she married Buddy Rogers in 1937 and they adopted Ronnie and Roxanne soon after that."

I wanted to ask why they adopted, to ask if Miss Pickford couldn't have children or what, but it didn't seem right. As I looked at the pictures, I already felt like I was intruding on her privacy somehow. I don't know why, really. She'd spent her life in pictures. But it felt like spying to me all the same.

April 2, 1979

Buddy told me years ago that I still cry out for Doug in my sleep sometimes. I felt a little bad, but I can't help it, can I? There's really nothing I can do about it. Jayar says I call Buddy 'Doug' sometimes now, too. Doug left me over forty years ago, and he's been dead almost forty years. And still my mind cries out his name, like a reflex almost, several times a day. Duber, I used to call him, and he used to call me Hipper. They were our private names for each other, but of course like everything else about a life in the public eye, they became known. I wonder if I'll see him again when my time comes? And after all these years, what will we say to each other?

I don't think Buddy could ever understand the connection Doug and I had. When we went to Europe on our honeymoon nobody was prepared for the crowds of fans. Nobody could have imagined before then that 300,000 people would turn out in London to see a couple of actors from moving pictures. We almost caused a riot in Paris, and when we returned, huge crowds showed up at railway stations all across the country on our way back to Hollywood. You can't have those kinds of unbelievable experiences with someone and not feel a very special connection to them. No one else can understand what living that kind of life is like.

More than that, we were the same kind of people — both grew up without fathers around, both had worked since childhood. He admired my drive, my independence. I loved his energy, his passion for life. Those swashbucklers and rogues he played on the screen, like The Thief of Bagdad and Zorro, weren't so far off from the real Doug. He was larger than life himself; never walked when he could leap, never chuckled when

The Poor Little Rich Girl

he could throw his head back and laugh from the diaphragm. I loved that about him.

My Oscars both sit on the shelf with the doll from Belasco. It gives me a great deal of satisfaction to think that one of mine was a competitive Oscar, Best Actress of 1929, while that son-of-a-bitch Chaplin just got two honoraries. If anybody should have died in 1939, it should have been him, not my Duber. Instead that miserable little man hung on until a year ago. What did Chaplin do after 1939 anyway but hang around with Communists and marry that poor idiot Oona O'Neill, a girl a third his age? Then, in the fifties, he went and sold all his shares in United Artists and didn't even tell me. Me, the only other remaining founding member!

I can't think about Chaplin anymore. He upsets me too much.

༄

Summer afternoons I noticed the greenish-brown cloud of haze over the city when the bus got onto the Hollywood Freeway. Some days it would be so hot and smoggy, the air would bear down on me like a weight, especially after working all day. I wondered if Miss Pickford felt the heat like that in Toronto, in Canada, back when she was still Gladys Smith. On the way to and from work I read a book I borrowed from Tony, a biography of Miss Pickford by a man called Robert Windeler. Los Angeles was all lemon groves when she first arrived here. Hard to imagine. Now in her air-conditioned bedroom in her mansion, cut off from the rest of the world, she lay slowly dying. At nine years old, the breadwinner in her family, as she toured with a stock company, rode crowded trains to play one-nighters in strings of little towns, could she have imagined where she'd end up? Could she have imagined where her hard work would take her? She knew what it was to work hard, and she did it for a long time. No wonder she was tired.

I showed Mama the book once. She couldn't believe the old lady I'd tell her about was the same beautiful girl with the blonde ringlets in the pictures. The publicity still of Miss Pickford from *A Good Little Devil*, made in 1914, looked like it was from another millennium, not just sixty years earlier.

"Ay, it's so sad, Maria. Don't you think so?"

"Everybody gets old, Mama, if they live long enough. And look at all the money she made. Look at everything she did, all the fame she had."

Mama shook her head. "Look at what she lost."

∽

April 10, 1979

People feel sorry for me now. They think I'm a lonely old lady waiting here in my room to die. That I have all the money and things I could ever want, but my life is over. They don't understand — this is exactly what I've always wanted. I have enough money that I'll never have to worry, and now I have all the privacy I didn't have when I was the most famous woman in the world. But even in the days when I made a million dollars a picture, I still always worried that it would suddenly dry up. I imagined Ma and my brother Jack and my sister Lottie and me on the street, and it would be my fault because I made a mistake.

The Poor Little Rich Girl

They're all long gone now. Ma died of cancer and Jack and Lottie died of drink. I could never have children of my own, thanks to that cheap abortion Ma put me up to in 1912. And me, a married woman — but I had no choice. She always hated Owen Moore, was thrilled when I divorced him later, Church or no Church. She knew that a baby right then would have ended my career, so that was that. I had no say in the matter. And Ronnie and Roxanne, I still don't know what went wrong with them. We never see either of them. Maybe Buddy and I were too old, too set in our ways to be parents by the time we adopted them. I don't know. Anyway, now I'm only responsible for myself. I can do as I please.

I don't understand how people could think I'm lonely. A great actress is never lonely. Dreams and illusions were my stock in trade, don't forget. I could make millions of people around the world believe I was a twelve year-old girl when I was over thirty. Yet I was a major force to be reckoned with, every studio executive in Hollywood knew that. With the stockpile of memories I have, with the imagination I have, do they really think I'm a lonely old bedridden lady? I am whoever it strikes my fancy to be, wherever, whenever I want. I am Kate from The Taming of the Shrew. *I am* Little Annie Rooney. *I am* Tess of the Storm Country. *I have dealt in the alteration of reality since I was five years old. If I want it to perpetually be my and Duber's wedding night in 1920, that beautiful night, it is, goddammit!*

It is.

∾

Near the end, we all knew Miss Pickford didn't have much time left. Most of the other staff had started to look for new jobs. Rita said she'd heard Dorothy Lamour needed two people, thought maybe we could get on there together and stay in Beverley Hills.

But I wasn't sure what I'd do when the job was over. Ramon's uncle had got him a good job in a machine shop in San Diego and he wanted me to come with him. I wanted to go. I wanted to leave East L.A., go out on my own with Ramon. I couldn't really imagine a future without him. The only problem was Mama. How could I tell her?

The minute they rushed Miss Pickford to Santa Monica Hospital that day, the place seemed empty and quiet, even though she almost never came out of her room. We knew she wouldn't be back. When she passed away a few days later, we all cried. Mr. Rogers kept us on staff for a few weeks after that to help clean Pickfair out, get it ready for sale. He'd already started to clear things out long before, didn't seem too sad when she finally died, I thought. But then it wasn't a surprise. She was old and very frail. And maybe it was a relief to him in some ways.

On the last day I helped Lupe finish the laundry. Then she and I helped some men move things out of Miss Pickford's room while Mr. Rogers supervised. When they took the mattress off her bed we found a small, black, leather-bound book on the box springs. Mr. Rogers picked it up and flipped through it.

"More garbage," he said. "Scribbling. Crazy old woman."

He threw the book into a trash can. Later, I fished it out. I didn't have to open it to know it was private, that Miss Pickford would have hidden it for a reason. I put it in my apron pocket and went back to work.

The Poor Little Rich Girl

As I waited for the bus back to East L.A. for the last time, I noticed the sweet smell of a cherry tree, like the one outside Miss Pickford's window. I'd never noticed there was one by the bus stop before. It was clear to me then. I had to tell Mama I was moving to San Diego with Ramon. If I didn't I'd regret it, maybe for the rest of my life. And I couldn't let Mama run my life — get me jobs, pick my boyfriends. I thought of Miss Pickford's mother putting her up to an abortion and shuddered. How different would her life have been if she'd stood her ground?

The bus was almost empty and I sat by a window and opened it up, felt the cool air on my skin. I took the book out of my pocket and flipped to the last entry. I do that sometimes, I'm the kind of person who can't wait to see how a book ends. For a moment I hesitated, wondered if this was too private, too painful. Maybe I shouldn't look at it. But then she wrote all this down to be read, didn't she? If Mr. Rogers didn't want to read it, I would. I'd at least try to make sense of it.

The last entry was written about two weeks before she died. The writing was very faint, large scratchy letters, hard to read. Her eyes were almost gone then, I guess. All it said was "Duber", over and over again, all down the page. It didn't make any sense. So I started back at the beginning. Someone owed that much to Miss Pickford.

The Selfish Professor

DYMPHNA SAT IN THE CHAIR DR. INNES offered and looked around nervously, folded her hands in her lap, tried to make them as inconspicuous as possible. He looked more or less the way she'd remembered him: pasty faced, receding reddish hair badly in need of a trim, and the requisite coke-bottle glasses. His office was tiny, cramped, messy. Books piled high on the desktop and every other available surface, filed haphazardly on the small shelf against the wall. A framed print of an elaborate mandala hung on the wall behind his desk, a photograph of Martin Buber hung on the opposite wall. He sipped out of a large coffee mug bearing the legend "World's Best Assistant Department Head" and consulted his desk calendar.

"Ms. Braun, is it?"

"Yes."

He cleared his throat. He'd spotted the mittens. And now he wondered why she wore them indoors on a warm spring day. "And what did you want to see me about?" he ventured, not taking his eyes off the thick grey wool.

The Selfish Professor

"Well. It's kind of unusual. You probably don't remember me, but I was in one of your first-year Religious Studies courses about ten years ago."

He squinted with the effort of recollection. "Sorry. I see so many students in just one year, never mind ten years ago . . ."

"I can imagine. Well, I guess I might as well get right to the point. What can you tell me about this?" She pulled off the mittens. Underneath, her hands were wrapped in strips of gauze. As she unwound these, he saw the bloodstains. In the palm of each hand was what appeared to be a raw, open wound, perhaps an inch in diameter. He muttered something under his breath.

"Pardon me?" she asked.

"I said, 'Who hath dared to wound thee?' It's from something I read a long time ago."

His hand slid a little closer to his desk phone. The raw, metallic smell of blood was now unmistakable. He fidgeted with his pen. "So, when did this happen?"

"About a month ago. I woke up one morning and there they were. They weren't as bad, early on, but the bleeding seems to be worse now. At first I was able to keep working — I'm with the public works department. But they've put me on short-term disability. Got me seeing a psychiatrist and all this stuff. They think I'm doing it to myself. Jesus."

"May I have a closer look?" he asked, timidly.

"Sure," she said. He rose, took her cold, white hands in his and inspected them, turned them over and over.

"Does it hurt?" he asked. He seemed unable to take his eyes off her hands. It made her uncomfortable and she wanted to put her mittens back on, hide behind them. Maybe disappear inside them.

"A little. Tylenol does a pretty good job though."

He sat back in his chair, silent for a few moments. She looked at him expectantly, assumed he was thinking her dilemma over, coming up with a solution. "So. What do you think?"

"What do I think? Well ... it certainly looks like stigmata."

"Yes, but I hoped you might be able to tell me what to do about them."

"I'm not sure what you mean."

"How do I get rid of them is what I mean. They're really getting to be a pain in the ass, if you'll pardon the expression. I can't work anymore. I get blood all over everything I own. What it's costing me in dry cleaning alone is insane. People think I'm crazy — my doctor, my friends, my co-workers. I even went to a priest. I mean, I haven't been inside a church in probably fifteen years, but I'm desperate. I figured if anybody would be able to help me, it'd be a priest. What a joke. He took one look, and I think he was just about ready to get sick on the spot. You'd think a guy who supposedly performs last rites and all that stuff wouldn't be so squeamish, but he turned green. He hustled me out of there and locked the door behind me, muttered something about marks of divine favour."

"I'm sorry. I don't know that there *is* anything you can do about it, although I'm not positive about that. They're fairly rare, you know. I've never seen stigmata up close."

"Pardon me, but could I have a couple of Kleenexes?" she asked, and nodded at the box on his desk.

"Oh, of course."

The Selfish Professor

She dabbed at the wounds, then re-wrapped the gauze around her hands. "I suppose *you* think I'm crazy, too." She slipped the mittens back on.

"Not at all. I find this quite fascinating."

"But you can't tell me why I got them? How I can get rid of them?" She stood now, ready to go.

"Well, not really. But listen, maybe we could discuss this further. Over dinner, perhaps?" Impulsively, he had taken her hands and caressed them through the grey wool. His grey eyes looked into hers. His face was flushed a blotchy pink, made his reddish eyebrows seem white. Strangely, she found the effect not wholly unattractive.

She jerked her hands away from him. "Dinner? Don't tell me you're turned on by this."

"It's just that I've never seen — I mean, I've never met anybody like you before."

"Oh, my God! I don't believe this." She stormed out of his office and started off down the hall. He caught up to her, grasped her upper arm.

"Don't go. I'm sorry. I don't know what came over me. Listen, maybe I can help you. I know someone at Ohio State University who's something of an authority on all things Catholic. I could give him a call, see what he has to say."

Dr. Innes did have a charming, boyish smile, she had to give him that. She found herself smiling back in spite of herself, perhaps because of his earnestness. It was probably a studied earnestness, she decided.

"Really?"

"If anybody can help you, it'll be him. It's too late now, otherwise I'd call him today, but I can call him first thing

129

tomorrow." They had turned around and headed back down the hall to his office.

"That would be great. And I'm sorry, too. It's just that things have been very strange for me the last little while. It seems like my life is falling apart."

"No need to apologize. I can't imagine. So, about dinner..."

"Seriously? Well, listen, before I say yes, I want to tell you that I tried to get help from your colleague, Dr. Robertson, last week. *He* wanted to take me out for Steak Tartare, the pervert."

"He did? How revolting. Robertson always was a little over the top. I've had my doubts about him for many years. In very poor taste. May I apologize on behalf of the Religious Studies department?"

Boyish, charming *and* he had manners. "Thank you. I'd love to have dinner with you."

"Great. How about sushi?"

Sisters of Mercy

OUT OF JAIL, OUT OF CIGARETTES, AND more than likely out of a job. What a lousy way to start the week. At least I'm out of jail, Rick thought as he jammed his hand into the breast pocket of his worn raincoat. He found five dollars, enough for a half-deck of smokes and a coffee to quell the pounding in his head and wash the wooly taste from his mouth. He raked his hand through his close-cropped dark hair, felt the four-day growth on his face.

It had all started Thursday night. Heading home after work he ran into Kirk, an old friend who'd been out of town working seismic the last few months. Kirk suggested they catch up over a beer and Rick had hesitated.

"I shouldn't."

"Aw, c'mon," Kirk persisted. "One beer. I'm buying."

Well, one beer. One free beer. No harm in that, was there? And he'd done well with that one free beer, had sipped it slowly while they caught up. The real trouble began when Kirk convinced him to have a shooter. "Just one," he'd said.

That was the end of Rick's good intentions that night. He and Kirk ended up closing the place down. The next day his hangover was enough to warrant calling in sick, but he felt he owed the sisters.

Mavis and Noreen weren't really sisters but Rick always thought of them as 'the sisters'. They were both grey-haired, both wore glasses. He got them mixed up a lot at first, but noticed after a while that Mavis was taller, Noreen pudgier. They were manager and assistant manager at the downtown Sisters of Mercy Thrift Shop. They'd worked side by side for ten years, had both been married to drinkers, had both been through divorces. After Rick's impaired conviction, he'd lost his job driving cab and had to work off his fine at the thrift store. When Noreen offered him a job, he knew it was mostly because she and Mavis wanted a man on the premises, someone to fend off the drunks and the guys who were off their meds. He found the idea that he could intimidate anyone laughable, but took the job until he could pick up something else.

Still, that morning he wished he'd stayed home. He poured himself a coffee, grunted a brusque hello, and watched Mavis and Noreen's reflections in the plate glass window that lined one wall of the workroom. He knew that Noreen noted the tremor in his hands, Mavis shook her head ever so slightly. These two would know just what a hangover looked like, no doubt about that. What would they say, then? Would the whole day be spent listening to little cracks about falling off the wagon? Questions about what he got up to last night? Hey, there was no law against going out for a few drinks with an old friend, was there?

Sisters of Mercy

He pulled a garbage bag full of donated clothes to his workstation, a long wooden table with a measuring tape along one edge for waistbands and inseams and stocked with pens, scissors, and price tags. He sat at the station nearest the window, Noreen had the middle station, and Mavis had the end one. Some people priced as they hung, but he liked to sort the whole bag first, then price. That way he got to look at the clothes twice in case he missed a tear or a stain. Things that were too dirty or damaged went into the garbage. Clean but torn items with a high cotton content were sold to painters as rags. Pretty much everything else went on the racks.

"I haven't noticed Annie Davis in the store lately," said Mavis. "Have either of you seen her?"

Annie Davis was a regular, someone all the staff knew to keep an eye on when she came in. She was slight, agitated, mostly moved in rapid jerks, seemed to have a hard time focusing on things. At first Rick had figured her age at mid-forties and was shocked when Doreen told him she was twenty-eight. "Street life and drugs age people fast," she'd said. Annie would either be in a change room putting on clothes under the ones she came in wearing, slipping small items into her pockets or talking rapidly and incomprehensibly to whoever was working cash. Mavis and Noreen had banned her from coming in many times, but always relented when Annie promised she was on her meds, swore she was trying hard.

"I haven't seen her in a while," said Rick. He didn't really feel like talking; his head had started to throb.

"The last time I saw her was a couple of weeks ago," said Noreen. "She tried a few times to get a red sweater we had in the window display but I kept my eye on her."

"She likes bright things," Mavis said.

Noreen nodded. "Anything bright or shiny. She kind of reminds me of a crow."

"She'll pick up anything that catches her eye," said Mavis. "You wonder what she does with it."

"I'll bet half the stuff doesn't even make it home with her. You know how scattered she is," said Noreen.

Mavis went out to the front for a while to help Danielle, the new girl who was working cash, with a voucher. The store honoured vouchers from various social service agencies who were helping clients through difficult times of one kind or another — job loss, addiction recovery, divorce, leaving abusive relationships. As long as the store had the clothes and small household items the vouchers usually called for, usually just the basics, they would provide them free of charge. This voucher must have been a big one, because it kept Mavis out of the workroom for quite a while.

Rick was grateful for the quiet. In the six months he'd worked there he'd never come in hung over before; it was the first time since his conviction he'd been drunk. They knew and he knew they knew. He did his work, counted the minutes until lunch, sure he'd feel better after he ate.

Lunch didn't help, though. If anything, he felt worse, probably because he'd started to think about money. As if being hung over wasn't bad enough, he had to worry about that. He'd never get ahead with this job, that much was obvious. He made just enough to pay his rent and eat and smoke. He couldn't save anything and he couldn't find another job. If he could just save a little, he'd move back to Saskatoon. He'd been in Calgary ten years and it was getting too big, too impersonal for him. Whatever attraction moving here had held for him had disappeared. He could barely remember what brought him in the first place. In Saskatoon he'd stay with Mom for a while, maybe even look up Ellen. Kirk said he'd heard she was single again. After ten years he was ready to forgive her. They'd only been lovers for a couple of months years ago before she told him, almost as an afterthought, that she was getting married in two weeks.

Mavis and Noreen were setting up a new display in the in the front window when he got back from lunch and Rick was grateful for the absence of their chatter in the workroom. He hung out a bag of men's suits and started to price them, thought about how he'd sleep when he got home, dive into the cool sheets and pass out. He was about to take the eight suits out to the rack on the floor when he remembered how Mavis scolded him the week before about not checking the pockets. He'd seen her this morning, checking some things he'd just hung out. He hated checking pockets. You never knew what you'd find: old Kleenexes, toothpicks, cigarettes, bus tickets, condoms, receipts, food, you name it.

He felt something in the breast pocket of the first suit, something bulky, dry, papery. He took out a thick roll of bills held together with an elastic band. After a long moment he slipped it into his jeans pocket, the blood pounding in his ears, his palms damp.

Rick went into the washroom, locked the door behind him. Four tens, five twenties, six fifties, and a hundred. Enough to get back to Saskatoon. He rolled it up, put the elastic around it, shoved it into his pocket and went back to the workroom.

As the afternoon dragged by, he thought about turning it over. But even if the person who donated the suit realized the money was missing, there would be no way to trace it. The clothing that Sisters of Mercy sold was either donated directly to the stores or to their warehouse, where it was sorted and distributed to the four locations. This suit came from a bag from the warehouse. It might have gone to any of the stores, the suit might have been thrown out during the preliminary sort at the warehouse. The suit could have belonged to someone who had passed on. Maybe the money sat in that pocket for years, long forgotten.

It didn't take long to make up his mind. The minute he got off work he'd go to his room in the crumbling, faded boarding house on 6th Street East, pack his things and leave. He had enough money to fly home, but he figured he'd be frugal and take the bus. That way he'd still have enough to live on for a week or so.

The afternoon finally ended. Mavis and Noreen, he had to hand it to them, hadn't said a single word all day about his being hung over. He felt a little sorry to leave them short come Monday morning, but he knew they could handle it. They were tough gals, these two. Mom would love to have him home while he got back on his feet and maybe he'd even enroll in university again, make a real go of it this time. And he'd look up Ellen. Definitely.

Out on the street he passed The Empress, where he and Kirk drank the night before. About a block further along, he remembered he was almost out of cigarettes and decided to go back to the newsstand. Once he was so close to The Empress, he thought he'd buy himself one drink to celebrate leaving this place and starting over. One drink, he thought as he descended the stairs into the beer parlor, then it's home to pack.

That much he remembered clearly. It got blurry after that, blurrier still until he woke up about four AM in the drunk tank. He didn't even realize until they released him at about 6:30 that it was Tuesday morning, not Monday morning. The weekend was gone and he had no idea what he'd done the whole time, although he was able to make some educated guesses. The money was gone: he'd managed to drink it all away.

Mavis and Noreen were plainly relieved when he walked in. They got up from their workstations and followed him into the office as he hung up his coat, both asked at once where he'd been.

"We called your landlady," Noreen said. "She said she hadn't seen you all weekend. We called the hospitals and we were going to call the police if you hadn't shown up this morning."

You should have called them, he thought. *They knew exactly where I was.*

"I'm really ashamed of myself. I fell off the wagon."

Mavis looked over her glasses at Noreen, Noreen looked back at Mavis. Rick cringed a little, waited for their response. Mavis spoke first. "It's all right. You're only human. Don't worry about it. Just let us know if you can't make it in to work again."

"There's no use beating yourself up about it. Just be careful," advised Noreen.

He assured them he would and thanked them, embarrassed, for their concern. He got a bag of clothes and started to hang them at his workstation. Sisters of Mercy, eh? There might be something to it, at that.

Beware of God

THE CROWD IN THE BOOKSTORE COMFORTED ME somehow. Comforted or numbed; either way, it worked. I'd only recently been able to go places again and hadn't been in a bookstore in a long time. The experience, amazingly, was much the same as before: browsers still stood in silence among the shelves you could disappear behind, the shelves that could swallow you up; staff still pushed trucks of new stock to shelve discreetly between customers. It was all the same. How could it be so, I wondered, and yet how could it be otherwise? The soft music, the heady aroma of coffee made me almost decide to sit and linger over a cup until my eye caught the familiar face of the tall man at the end of the aisle. After a mutual flicker of recognition I realized it was Bill Howard, my assistant. He smiled, briefly, timorously, the tight, forced smile of a man who does not really want to smile at all.

"Hello, Marian."

"How've you been?"

"I'm well. I'm well. We've missed you."

The auburn haired, freckled woman behind him was his wife, I remembered. I'd met her at Christmas parties over the years. What was her name? I'd never think of it right now. But she was with him, just as I'd feared, and she wheeled a stroller up behind him.

"Marian, do you remember Janis? And this is our daughter, Kayla."

Kayla looked to be about a year old. Oblivious to her parents and me, she squealed and wriggled, got her chubby, sticky hands all over a display of Robert Ludlum paperbacks. I found I couldn't look at her anymore, but I could tell by the way Janis averted her eyes, nearly winced when I looked at her, that the blurring and the stinging heat of my approaching tears were no longer secret. I looked away, too.

I pulled out of it with some chit-chat, all parties involved relieved when it was over, particularly Kayla. I found the washroom and checked myself in the mirror, surprised at how composed I looked: mascara not running, nose and eyes not red. Only a hard glitter to the eyes that might give me away. That and maybe a certain long-standing, habitual set of the jaw.

There's got to be someone to blame, and I'm still firmly mired in the blaming stage, so I blame Russ, or his mother. Actually, they can share the blame: he's the one who insisted on the whole church business in the first place and she's the one who guilted him into it. Pair of hypocrites, the both of them. She's about as Christian as Attila the Hun and the only time Russ ever thought about religion before that was at funerals. Even then, he used to snarl about the stupidity of it all for days afterwards. So you can imagine my surprise when he made noises, one Sunday morning, about going to church. Naturally, I thought he was kidding so I just played along.

"Okay. Which one? Why don't we go to the Church of God over on forty-fifth? Church of God, like there's some other kind of church."

"I meant St. Barnabas."

"Sure, but why limit ourselves? We could hit them one week, the Catholics the next . . . "

"Marian. I'm serious."

I put my crossword puzzle down, looked at him over my reading glasses, wondered for a brief, terrifying moment if he'd had some brush with mortality. He had just been for a checkup a couple of weeks earlier. Maybe they'd found something he hadn't told me about yet. Or maybe it was mid-life crisis, "andropause," whatever they call it these days.

"What's wrong?"

"There's nothing wrong. It's just that Mom's getting on. You know she hasn't been so well lately."

Russ's mother had been dying since the day I met her in 1971. I think it's her very ill health that keeps her going. Well, ill health and haranguing Russ. "How exactly will our going to church improve things for her?"

"It would just make her feel better. She worries, not about us so much, more about Jennifer."

Jennifer. Suddenly, the light bulb came on. "It's the sign, isn't it?"

"No. Well, actually it did make me think about it, I guess."

A couple of years earlier, Jennifer had hung a sign on the outside of her bedroom door, the kind you get in hardware stores with fluorescent orange letters on a black background, that read, "NO TRESPASSING". Recently, she'd replaced it with one that said, "BEWARE OF DOG", only she'd cut out the letters in the last word and reversed them. I thought it was kind of funny.

"I don't think it means our daughter has become a Satanist. She just has a fondness for wordplay. Anyway, good luck getting her out of bed anytime before noon on a Sunday. As for me, I see no reason to spend my Sunday mornings in an institution that you have disparaged for years for the sole purpose of making your mother happy."

"I just thought, you know, she might not be around much longer and it would be such a small effort . . . "

He stroked his greying beard as he spoke; he was nervous. The poor dear. It wasn't so much us going to church that would make the old so-and-so happy, it would be the simple act of submission to her will that would satisfy her. "We could just tell her we've been going. To a different church, of course, not St. Barnabas, otherwise she'd know."

"We could *not* do that."

"Why not? They don't take attendance, do they?"

"If you're going to be sarcastic, I don't think there's any point in having this conversation."

"Look, I'm sorry, but come on. The man who's rejected organized religion as superstitious nonsense as long as I've known him all of a sudden tells me he's found God? I mean, the first thing that came to my mind was that it must be a joke."

"I didn't say I'd found God. I just said it would make my mother happy in the last part of her life if we showed up at church now and again. And it's not a joke."

Turns out the joke was on me. We were in St. Barnabas the next Sunday.

∞

Just because Russ and I went didn't mean Jennifer would. Russ was annoyed by her complete lack of interest. I saw him glare, as he tried to argue with her, at her blue-black, lawnmower-cut hair, her piercings, her clothes, all topics of dispute between them in the past.

Jennifer wasn't having any of it. She looked at Russ and shrugged. "I'd rather visit Oma than go to church to make her happy," she said and suddenly the discussion was over. How could this wise, calm creature be a child of mine, I wondered as she descended the basement stairs to her bedroom to answer the phone.

"She's down there all the time," Russ muttered. "When she's not hanging out with her friends with all their tattoos and their piercings. I think she spends an awful lot of time in her room."

"She does. I suppose you didn't when you were a kid."

"I don't think I was in my room *that* much. Whenever she's at home she's down there, listens to that God-awful music she's into, all about death and despair. I only see her at meals. And not even all the time then."

"Should she come up here and dig The Grateful Dead with us? At her age, she'd rather be on the phone with her friends than with her parents. I was the same way."

∞

Since I've been off work I've managed to avoid most people, people outside family and close friends, that is. I think particularly of some of my co-workers, and I'm afraid they'll ask questions. Frankly, I'm in no shape to talk about it. Not that most decent people would ask, I'm sure. But you never know, and I just don't want to take that risk yet, even though I suppose they've probably all heard by now. Most days it's hard enough to talk to Russ or his mother about it; talking to people outside the family, I break down. So the only thing I've arrived at is avoidance. It's not much of a coping strategy, but it's all I've got.

∞

We started to attend services at St. Barnabas, as I said. Regular church attendance hadn't been part of my life since my early teens. But I found the standing, the sitting, the kneeling, all at the same prescribed times, the singing, even the words, were almost identical in the Anglican services and the Catholic Masses of my girlhood. To think people had fought and died over the ridiculous little differences.

Russ told me I didn't have to come with him if I didn't want to. I would have loved to stay home with my tea and my slippers and my paper, but it was bad enough to listen to him make excuses for Jennifer: she had a bad cold, she had an essay to turn in the next day, she had to study for finals. I didn't have the heart to make him dream up alibis for me too. He couldn't just tell his mother that Jennifer and I weren't into organized religion, that he wasn't either for that matter. Much as I would have loved to hear him say it, much as I would have liked to see her mouth purse up and her moony little face turn red.

I went with him, but that was as far as I would go. I would not be a party to nagging Jennifer.

"Jennifer is seventeen. I think she's old enough to decide whether she wants to go to church or not, don't you?"

He was touchy the rest of the evening. Maybe that wasn't the answer he wanted to hear, but it was the truth. People should listen to the truth, I thought, instead of pressuring other people to say and do what they wanted them to. Because eventually the truth will out, or at least you hope so. Because you get so damn tired of listening to these little white lies designed to spare people's feelings, or whatever it is they're supposed to accomplish. Russ's mom eventually stopped asking why Jennifer wasn't there, like she figured it out, or finally decided it wasn't worth wasting any more of her nagging power on.

∽

One Sunday a couple of months later we returned from church for what turned out to be the last time. We changed out of what had become our church clothes and Russ went downstairs to ask Jennifer what she wanted for lunch. I peered into the fridge, tried to decide whether to heat up last night's lentil soup or make sandwiches, when he bounded up the stairs. He looked at me, said nothing, breathed very hard from the unaccustomed effort of running. He looked at me, yet he looked at nothing, or at something far off, or at something he still saw in his eyes that wouldn't go away.

I had no idea she was even depressed. She'd always been the serious type, quiet, and she did spend a lot of time in her room on the phone. Didn't all teenagers? In those first few weeks after it happened, I kept saying, "If only we'd been home . . ." not realizing, in my grief, how little sense that made.

Not many of her friends have come to visit. Shannon's her best friend and even she's only been by a couple of times. I think it all terrifies them. I'm just starting to get used to it myself. Things like the smells — the antiseptic smell, the metallic smell of blood, so foreign at first, yet something I encounter now every day, associate now with her. So strange. What remains is the thing everyone thinks but no one articulates. The elephant in the room, so obvious, taking up all the space and crushing the furniture, but no one talks about it. No one has to. I think it all the time, and I hate myself for thinking it, but I can't help thinking it: this is worse than death. As she lies in this bed, unresponsive, unseeing, caught in a snarl of tubes and gauges, I think it's not really Jennifer.

I think that, and then sometimes I want to slap myself for thinking it. Because this is Jennifer, *this is Jennifer*, something inside me screams. The real Jennifer. Not the Jennifer I thought I knew, not the Jennifer who yakked on the phone about cute boys or whatever it was I figured she yakked about. I guess the thing was I had no idea what she talked about, what she thought about, who she really was. But this is who she is now. Now it's all clear enough.

Bells and Whistles

I COULD MELT HOLES WITH MY BREATH in the ice that formed around the bottom of the windowpane. I'd kneel over the back of the chair up against the window and breathe a row of holes. The little pools of water on the windowsill smelled like wet dust. I'd watch the stars, look out at the diamonds glinting on the snow under the streetlights by the tracks. I watched cars, trains, the few people out on the street, maybe a dog nosing around in the alley. Looking out the window was the only thing I could do, the only safe thing, anyway. I really wanted to read, but then I'd have to have a light on. I'd have to have a light on and I'd have to look at the book, which would mean I couldn't also look out the window. Once, I got all interested in *Little Women* and forgot to watch out the window. After that I decided that the only safe thing to do was look out my bedroom window in my pajamas with the lights off.

I guess I could have just gone to bed, but I usually couldn't fall asleep until Mom got home. Sometimes I could, but most of the time I'd be too worried to sleep until I was sure she was back. But she'd get mad if she knew I was awake. I tried to explain to her that I hated being left alone. She'd just get madder. "Just *don't* worry," she'd advise me, and slip on her navy wool coat and black gloves all the same, no matter how I protested. "What do you think will happen to you, anyway? Just go to sleep and then you won't have to think about it." She'd give me a kiss, take a last look at her hair in the mirror by the front door, reapply Cherries in the Snow and be gone.

༄

Miriam Kalman sat in front of me at school. She wore cat's-eye glasses from when her sister was in third grade, passed on like a precious heirloom, probably with the same prescription. What surprised me was that she hadn't found some way to write her name on them like she had on everything else she owned. MIRIAM K., in towering, shaky block letters, was on her books, her desk, her lunchbox, the tags of all her sweaters and jackets, and in red on both her runners. MIRIAM K., MIRIAM K., they proclaimed each by each, like there might be some other marauding Miriam around just waiting for the chance to get her hands on those white canvas runners.

Miriam was an okay person to have in front of you. She wasn't one of those people who would blather on until the teacher came over, getting you both in trouble. Miriam would pass notes quietly, talk when it was safe to do so, and generally share candy if she had any. I didn't mind sitting behind her at all.

I'd recently discovered that Miriam was a reader, too. We both shelved books in the school library Tuesday lunch hours and got to talking books as we shelved a truckload of fiction. She also loved some of my favourites: *Island of the Blue*

Bells and Whistles

Dolphins by Scott O'Dell, *Lassie Come Home* by Eric Knight, *All-of-a-Kind Family* by Sydney Taylor.

"We should go to the main library downtown, sometime. Maybe on a Saturday afternoon," she said.

"Main library?"

"You know. The big public library downtown."

"I haven't been there." Actually, I vaguely remembered being there once when I was very little. Mom had needed to talk to someone at the reference desk and she told me to sit still at a table and wait until she was done.

"Oh, you'd love it, Angie. Six floors full of books. You mean you don't even have a library card?"

"No."

"Well, we have to go."

"Yeah. I'd like that a lot."

∾

Mom used to complain about the trains, said she wanted to move someplace where the noise wouldn't keep her up all night. It never bothered me. I liked the sound. I guess it was because we'd lived in that apartment as long as I could remember, since shortly after Dad had died, but I found the sounds of the bells, the whistles, the shunting kind of soothing. Lots of times they were the sounds that lulled me to sleep at last.

She also said that Mrs. Kurtz next door drove her nuts. Maybe Mrs. Kurtz was just lonely, I don't know, or maybe she just liked to talk. But she was forever dropping by, or would catch us as we were going in or out and start talking. A snoop, Mom said, a busybody. Sometimes Mom would get fed up with the trains and Mrs. Kurtz, and make noise about moving. She'd circle ads in the paper, but as far as I could tell that was all she ever did about it.

∽

Mrs. Behr looked kind of green. The principal had knocked on the door and asked to speak to her outside. She told us to do some silent reading, which of course was our cue to act up. She was only gone for a few minutes but we'd already raised the noise level to a respectable roar by the time she came back. Normally, she would have had to yell at us and threaten us with extra homework before we quieted down. This time we knew something was up, though. She sat down at her desk, looked at nothing.

"There's been an accident," she said after a while. "Miriam was killed in accident."

I stared at the seat in front of me, empty for three days.

∽

I never did get the details straight. Mrs. Behr said a train hit Miriam on her way home from school on Monday, but as the days went by numerous versions of the story went around the school. I suppose, in the days before grief counselors, this was how people dealt with tragedy: by making up stories about it. First, we heard that she'd got her foot stuck in the tracks and they'd found her body sliced into a thousand pieces, the snow soaked all around like a cherry Slush. Then we heard that she got dragged screaming under the wheels for twenty miles and that was why it took so long to find her. Then it came out that she'd almost made it across, but the train threw her skinny little body into the railroad crossing signpost and broke her neck. Someone else said she'd fallen asleep on the tracks and never knew what hit her. In many versions of the story, Miriam's second-hand glasses were clearly to blame for her fatal lack of judgment. It was hard to know what to believe.

"Awful about that poor little girl," Mrs. Kurtz had said when I came home after school one day. "Did you know her?"

"She sat in front of me in class."

"Oh, I'm so sorry, Angie. What a terrible thing."

The sad look on Mrs. Kurtz's face alone was enough to make me feel like crying, never mind thinking about Miriam. My eyes started to tear up and I fumbled with the front door key. "It is. Terrible. Excuse me, Mrs. Kurtz. I have some homework."

∽

"Angie? You still up?" Mom was furious that I was still awake when she got home. She must have seen the yellow crack of light under my door and burst in, still in her coat.

"I can't sleep. I wanted to ask you something about purgatory."

"Listen to me. Your little friend is in heaven. Never mind what those stupid kids at school said about purgatory. Purgatory is only for sinners, and Protestants, I think, under certain circumstances. Miriam was only eight — how could she have sinned? Now don't worry about it. She's with the angels, happy as can be."

I seldom found Mom very reassuring.

∽

It wasn't long after Miriam died that the dreams started. I didn't have them every night, but I had them pretty regularly, mostly on nights Mom was out. I was always in my bed asleep and then I woke up and smelled smoke. I got out of bed and felt the door, like they told us to at school, and it was hot. Smoke seeped in under the door. I went to the window and tried to open it, but it was stuck shut. I started to scream, tried to yank the window open, and that was always when I woke up.

Once I asked Mom why she left me alone. She didn't do it every night, it's true. But Friday and Saturday for sure, and sometimes once or twice during the week. It wasn't even until I got into school and started to meet other kids that it occurred to me that there was anything out of the ordinary about my mother going out at nights and leaving me by myself. I thought it was something that all kids had to deal with and that I was a baby because I didn't like it. When I was little, I know Grandma was around, but she died when I was five. After that, Mom just told me to read until 8:30 and then get into bed. I wasn't allowed to read all night because she was not an irresponsible mother, I guess. Don't answer the door, she said. It was okay to answer the phone, though I wasn't to tell anybody that I was alone. Instead, I was just supposed to say that Mom couldn't come to the phone right now.

Anyway, when I asked her why, I was instantly sorry I asked.

"Look. I work all week to support you. I have no husband to help me with anything. Do you think it's easy raising a child alone? Why the hell shouldn't I go out and enjoy myself for a few hours?"

Bells and Whistles

By this time I knew better than to say anything else. She was set off already. So I said nothing, just nodded, and she continued. "You're old enough to stay by yourself for a few hours, aren't you? You have the brains not to set the place on fire or anything like that, I'm sure. And I don't have any money to give to a babysitter, so you'd better just get used to it. Besides, if there's ever really an emergency you can always go to old Mrs. Kurtz next door."

That was what Mom was like. Sometimes I wondered if she'd always been that way, or had it just started after Dad died? I was too little to remember. When she said something, that was it. No questions. If I was dumb enough to start with the questions, she'd get really mad. Even so, there were times I thought about going to Mrs. Kurtz. I almost did once. I don't even know what spooked me that night. I was just lying there, listening to the trains like always. Then my hands and feet went ice cold, my insides knotted up, and it was all I could do not to run over to 308 screaming for Mrs. Kurtz.

But I made myself ride it out, even as I stood there with one hand on the doorknob to our apartment and bit the nails of the other hand. I stood there and let the fear shake me until I calmed down enough to consider what might happen. Was this a real emergency? Was the apartment on fire, was a maniac trying to break in, was I gravely ill? No. I considered what might happen if, just because I was afraid, I told Mrs. Kurtz I was alone in our apartment. There must be some rule, some law against leaving children alone, otherwise why would Mom not want anyone to know? So she'd be sent to prison. And then what would I do? I couldn't even sell matches like in Hans Christian Andersen, not in this day and age, with lighters being cheap and plentiful. Besides, I was sure there was some kind of law against child labour, too. Worse, I thought about what Mom would do when they eventually let her out of prison.

I crawled back into my bed.

∞

My eyes opened to blackness. My heart pounded a million tiny beats a minute, like a hamster's. I heard banging on the front door and my first sleep-addled idea was that it was Mom, keys forgotten. But it wasn't Mom; it was Mrs. Kurtz.

"Angie, are you okay?" I was too sleepy to even form an answer yet. "I heard screaming — was that you?"

I stood there silent, fumbled for an answer when Mom came up behind Mrs. Kurtz. "What's going on here?" she wanted to know.

"That's what I'd like to know, Anne," Mrs. Kurtz said. "It's three in the morning, your daughter is screaming with nightmares and where are you?"

"Out getting her some medicine, of course."

"Getting her some medicine? Where would you get medicine at this time of night? Reilly's Beer Parlor?"

I expected Mom to rip into her, like she would have done to me if I'd been foolhardy enough to make such a remark to her. "Don't be ridiculous," she said, and slipped by Mrs. Kurtz and into the apartment. "Now it's time we got you back into bed, miss. Sorry about the disturbance, Sylvia."

She closed the door, hung up her coat, and then grabbed me by the collar of my pajamas.

"Don't you ever do that again," she told me through clenched teeth.

"I didn't do it on purpose. I was having a bad dream."

"You wouldn't have bad dreams if you didn't waste so much time reading that garbage you've always got your nose stuck in. Now get back to bed."

∽

After that, things were different. For quite a while, she talked about moving away from meddling neighbours. We even went to look at a couple of new apartments, but anything we could afford was either too small or not close enough to work. Eventually, she gave up on the idea.

She also stayed in nights after that. It was a little strange having her around all the time. I still did my homework right after school, had a bath after supper. After my bath, Mom would want us to do something together. If I picked up a book she'd say, "Do you want to waste your whole life reading? C'mon and we'll play cards." After a time, she came to accept that I was just not a card player. We tried board games for a while, which I find only slightly more interesting than cards. After the board game phase, she insisted we spend the evenings watching some TV together. Bedtime was still stood unwavering at 8:30. This went on all through the winter and into the spring.

The nightmares stopped for a long time, but when I did eventually have one, Mom was right there to reassure me. Then I remembered that she probably rushed to my side because she was afraid of waking Mrs. Kurtz. Whatever her motives were, she was trying, I knew that. Maybe she still wasn't a great parent, probably not even a good one, but I think she was doing all she knew how to do.

One May evening, she stood and looked out the window after I came out from my bath. The day had been warm, a soft breeze blew in through the partly opened window.

"Go out if you want to," I said.

"What?"

"Go out if you want to. I don't mind."

"I wouldn't be long. Just a couple of hours."

"It's all right. Go."

It took her less than five minutes to change, fix her makeup and get her coat on. "Are you sure you don't mind?" she asked.

"Go ahead."

She wished me goodnight and I listened as her heels clicked down the hall and into the stairwell.

I settled into the chair by the window, watched her walk around the corner and out of sight. I opened the new book I'd borrowed from the main library, *Treasure Island*, and listened to the familiar bells and whistles outside. Before long I was lost to the words and didn't notice them anymore.

Ghost Rag

CLARA AND GEORGE WATCH a *Tom and Jerry* DVD while I crash on the couch behind them, feet propped on the coffee table, about to go unload the dishwasher before I make their lunches and get them to bed. But I'm too exhausted to move. The kids lie side by side in front of the TV, entranced, dark heads in hands, and any second now George's foot moving in time to the music will hit the half-empty glass of juice he's left on the rug.

"Finish your juice and put the glass on the table," I say. He doesn't listen.

"George!"

"What?"

"Finish your juice!"

"Okay, okay."

In this cartoon Tom is a concert pianist wearing a tux with the '40s-style padded shoulders and wide lapels. He plays Liszt's "Hungarian Rhapsody #2" while Jerry torments him. Jerry slams the lid on Tom's fingers, pulls out the felt hammers and smacks Tom with them, puts mousetraps on the keyboard; the usual Jerry kind of stuff. I listen to the music and look over at my own piano. The thick layer of dust that covers it is barely visible among the cards, which I should put away, and the wizened, dried-up flowers, which I should throw out. Dust even covers the keyboard, I'm ashamed to admit. It hasn't been touched in God knows how long.

Sometimes, like right now, my fingers actually ache to play. But when have I had time lately — when will I? The only time I could conceivably play is after they're in bed, and then I can't because I'd wake them up. If I had money I'd buy an electric piano like we have at the store, and play with headphones on, much as the idea offends me. But I don't have the money, and anyway, why should I buy one when I've got a perfectly good upright? A big, dusty, upright flowerstand. It shouldn't even have flowers on it, I know. What if a vase spills and water gets in the works, or ruins the finish? But where else am I supposed to put them? And it doesn't matter if it gets wet, anyway. No one ever plays the damn thing anymore.

"Mom! George spilled his juice!" Clara points to the upturned glass, the spreading orange pool on the rug.

"George! I *told* you to be careful, didn't I? Don't just stand there! Go and get me a rag," I snarl, and swat him on the backside to hurry him up. George bolts to the hall closet and brings me a rag. I don't want to scream at him but I can't stop. "Turn off the TV and brush your teeth, both of you! And get into bed. Why do you have to make more work for me?"

"Sorry," he whines.

I wipe up the juice, get a drink of water, listen to the tap run in the bathroom as they brush their teeth. Now the shame creeps up. I know it was an accident.

Ghost Rag

What's happening to me?

∼

When I think about it now, everything seemed to lead to it, one way or another. For instance, Clara and George and I were in the dollar store on a rainy day when I found a cheap-looking CD called *Scott Joplin's Greatest Hits*. I almost didn't buy it, but I'm a sucker for ragtime piano. It turned out to be the most amazing CD, performed by John Arpin, a collection of rags by Joplin, Eubie Blake, Jelly Roll Morton, W.C. Handy, Gershwin. And William Bolcom's elegant, melancholy 1971 *Graceful Ghost Rag*. It inspired me to put a hold on a collection from the library, *William Bolcom: The Complete Piano Rags* which included a suite of three Ghost Rags. The liner notes talked about how Bolcom and his friends wrote rags for each other in the '60s and '70s. He wrote *Graceful Ghost* for his late father.

I whistled parts of it, picked out bits on the keyboard when I had a second in between going to the hospital and taking the kids back and forth to school. That was about the last time I played at all.

∼

My hours at McAuley's Music are flexible, which means I work the hours no one else will. But Martin, my boss, was good to me when David got sick. He let me have all the time off I needed and covered for me at a moment's notice. He even invented a bogus inventory project for extra cash when I had to let my students go.

Sometimes Dora from the day home down the street picks up the kids, sometimes I go there to get them. I feel out of place as I stand in the hall with the other moms who know each other. Though we've lived here almost a year, with everything that's happened I haven't met many people. Besides, I don't have time or the energy for the gossip, the complaints about the weather. I stand off to one side, don't talk to any of them as I wait for George and Clara. She's always so poky — just like David. It drives me nuts.

"Mom, can we go to the playground for a while after school?" Clara asks when she finally shows up.

"Not today."

"Why not?" George asks.

"I've got all kinds of things to do today."

"We never go anymore," Clara says.

"I know. I've just been so busy. Maybe later in the week we can go."

All I want to do right now is go home and have some tea. If we hang around the playground, I'll have to chit-chat and I just can't do that right now. Maybe I want this to be the one place I don't have to think about it. Maybe I want this to be the one place where it isn't true.

∾

On a Sunday I am awakened by banging cupboard doors, pots and pans clanging, the repeated slamming of the fridge door. Clara stands in the middle of the kitchen, eyes wild, breathing hard. For just a moment she scares me.

"Clara. What's the matter?"

"Don't we have any waffles?" she demands.

Ghost Rag

"I don't know. Did you look in the freezer?"

"Of course I did."

"Well, that would be the only place we'd have frozen waffles. What's all the slamming and banging about?"

"I just can't believe we are out of waffles again."

"I can't believe you woke me up like that because we're out of waffles. You can have toast or cereal for breakfast."

She grumbles, puts bread in the toaster, won't talk to me for a while. At first I had thought that the kids were handling it well. After the initial shock of the diagnosis we all seemed to pull ourselves together, carried on as best we could, faced what we had to face. Or so I thought. But now I'm starting to think they're hiding their feelings to a large extent. From me, I guess, and maybe even more from themselves. But I'm starting to notice little things. Like Clara and her temper. She was always the one who'd fly off the handle most easily, but now it's much worse. And George has always whined, but I'm noticing it more and more now. What do I do?

∽

I don't want to think about David. I don't want to, but of course I can't think of anything else. Everything seemed to lead to it, like I said before. But maybe that's because right now I see everything through the prism of David, of what happened to him. It's a warm, sunny day in early October, the kids are at school and I've got a day off. Well, "off", kind of. I'm catching up with housework. How is it that there seems to be more now? I fold the laundry, listen to some music, look out the window. The sky seems bigger and bluer than just a week ago because the leaves have fallen in gold and amber piles on the grass and when you look up all you can see is sky through the branches. Gershwin's *Second Prelude* comes on and I smile, follow its slow, sensuous amble. Then I remember, and I can't enjoy it anymore. I keep thinking how Gershwin died when he was only thirty-nine, how David wasn't even thirty-nine. I start to hate the music, hate Gershwin, hate David, for ruining such a beautiful day. And then I feel guilty. Like it was anybody's fault. Like it was Gershwin's fault my husband died.

Something that's been really strange about all this is that until now, there's always been some kind of music. If I'm not playing it myself or listening to a recording, it's running through my head, on my mind, at my fingertips. And it's always matched my mood, or enhanced it. But now whatever I listen to seems to just make it worse, lead me back to David again. Gershwin, Mozart, Schubert, all of them dying so young. And let's not forget Chopin, another one who died at thirty-nine. Chopin's *Funeral March* is about the only music that gets stuck in my head these days. That or words. Words David said to me, or I said to him. Sometimes things I wish I hadn't said. Things I should have said, but didn't. But that's something new. It was always music before.

I pop the Gershwin disc out of the player and put it away. I don't want to hear it, don't even want to look at it. As I put the clothes away and for the rest of the day, the *Second Prelude* runs through my head. Gets stuck in my brain. I don't think I'll ever want to hear that disc again. I think I would have even preferred to stick with Chopin's *Funeral March*.

∽

My sister Jill calls from Ottawa, asks how things are.

"All right, I guess."

"How are the kids?"

"They seem pretty subdued, especially George. It probably hasn't sunk in yet."

"I guess it'll take some time. Leila, you ought to move out here, you know."

"Why would I want to do that?"

"There's more going on here than in Calgary, you've said so yourself. The kids could hang out with Sarah and James."

"I guess it's a possibility."

After I get off the phone with her I notice my shoulder feels sore. From holding the phone with it while I was putting the dishes away, probably. As I make lunches, Jill's words anger me. Why can't she just leave me alone for a while? Why does she have to get after me right away, tell me I ought to move out there? Haven't our lives been torn apart already as it is?

I just want everybody to leave me alone.

∽

One night after the kids were in bed, David sat and watched an old movie on TV. "Do you know what this is?" he asked.

He'd been home for a while by then. He was "finished work", as he'd been telling people. Which was true, but why did he have to be so blunt about it, so grim? He spent most of his time watching TV, which I thought was a huge waste. He didn't see it that way; he saw it as a way to keep his mind off things. But what does it matter now? It was his life, and that was what he wanted to do with the end of it.

I watched the movie for a few seconds. "It's *Dark Victory*. I saw it when I was a kid. Bette Davis has some kind of terminal disease or something. And Humphrey Bogart has the worst Irish brogue. You didn't see him doing that again."

I went to the kitchen and got us a couple of beers and sat down with him. Maybe we'd have a chance to relax a little together, enjoy a corny old movie. I'd forgotten what Bette Davis' illness was, but soon it became clear that it was a brain tumour. Of course, what else would it be? I looked over at David and saw the muscles in his cheek ripple.

"We don't have to watch this," I said.

"It's okay, I'm enjoying it."

We did relax after a while and started to make our usual cracks: David's about how Bette Davis looked like a frog, mine about how one of her hats resembled a reservoir tip. Bogart's brogue was even worse than I'd remembered. And the Hollywood death scene, where she suddenly becomes all backlit and soft-focused and flutters her false lashes and then the screen fades to black, was truly terrible.

David had his surgery in the summer, after piano lessons at the house were over, two months after they discovered the tumour. I told my students I'd given up teaching. The noise would have bothered David, seeing him would have bothered them. By the fall, when lessons would have started again, he was gone.

∽

Another mom sits next to me on one of the kid-sized chairs in the hallway across from George's classroom. She's round-faced and blonde.

"Hi. I'm Ruth Dexter, Braden's mom."

"I'm Leila Thompson."

"Oh, you're George's mom. He's such a little cutie. Nice boy."

"Thanks. I don't really know Braden. I don't get a chance to come into the classroom."

"Have to work?"

Before I know it, I tell her I was widowed a few weeks ago, that it's been a huge adjustment for all of us. I can see in my peripheral vision that other moms arrive now, too, stand on either side of us against the cinderblock walls. Are they listening? It doesn't really matter, I guess. My words sound for a while like someone else's voice. Someone friendly, someone normal, someone I don't know.

"That's terrible. I'm so sorry to hear that. Listen, I know people say this all the time, but if there's anything I can do . . . Maybe George could come over after school sometime?"

"That would be nice."

George and Clara finally gather up all their stuff and we start home. We haven't gone more than a few yards when George asks if we can please go to the playground.

"For a little while."

I find a bench and sit, feel the sun on my skin melt the tension out of my shoulders. Gershwin's *Second Prelude* winds its way through my head. I'm going to sit down at the piano and pick it out when we get home.

Close to the Bone

"THAT'S THE DEATH RATTLE," THE NURSE SAID in response to the look of confusion, of horror on my face. Her words surprised me, shook me a little. She said it like I'd been asking her where to find the washroom. I suppose she must have told others the same thing all the time, since she worked in palliative care. Funny, I've thought of that nurse many times over the years. What I always come back to is her teeth. They were prominent, nicely-shaped, and I couldn't stop looking at them because traces of something yellow stuck between the upper ones. I kept wondering if it was it plaque or food. She's a nurse, I thought, why does she have stuff on her teeth? It made no sense.

She drew the curtain around the bed then, said she'd just be a minute. "Why don't you get yourself a cup of tea?"

I went to the nourishment station down the hall, filled a Styrofoam cup with hot water, dropped in a tea bag and a cube of sugar ("white death" Charlotte would say), and squirted in lemon juice from a little packet. At home I took my tea black, but the tea here needed help, something to hide the turpentine taste. Normally, I wouldn't drink it in the middle of the night, either, but I needed a way to fight the brain-fog I'd had going on for the last couple of weeks. Tea probably wouldn't help, I knew, but I couldn't do much else right then.

When I got back, I took Charlotte's hand. Around her frail, almost transparent fingers, mine looked fat, deep pink, like they belonged to a cartoon character, Porky Pig maybe. The room was filled with the sound of her laboured breathing, each breath, you could tell, an agony, punctuated sometimes by this death rattle. I should have thought to ask more about it. Did it mean the moment was near? Should I try to get hold of Ian? Or would they do that? If I got up to go to the bathroom, would she be gone?

Later, another nurse woke me up. She said I should go home and get some sleep, they'd call if she started to go suddenly. The sound still gurgled out of her throat as I left the room. I wondered if this was the world's record for the longest death rattle. It was just starting to get light as I drove home.

~

We were both nineteen. Charlotte stood at the bottom of our steps with a backpack slung over her shoulder, the breeze lifted long strands of her light-brown hair over her slim shoulders. The grey stripes of her T-shirt brought out the flecks in her eyes. She was getting a ride with our neighbour as far as Revelstoke, then she planned to hitch to Vancouver. She'd been talking about going for weeks, but now that she was really doing it I felt miserable.

"I can't believe you're really going."

"You're just sad 'cause now there'll be one less person to split the rent."

"You know that's not true."

She kicked at the dirt awhile. "C'mon, Miriam. I'm kidding. I didn't think you'd miss me."

"Of course I will."

"Come with me, then."

"I can't just drop everything and go."

"Why not? What's keeping you here?"

Jay's truck pulled up. She threw her arms around me. "Keep in touch," I told her. "And be careful."

She wrote a few times, called a few times. After a couple of years, we lost track of each other. I knew she drifted for a while, from Vancouver to San Francisco and finally to Seattle, where she stayed almost five years.

One night her brother Ian called.

"Charlotte's back in town. She's sick. She wants you to come to see her."

She never could have afforded to be sick down there because she didn't have insurance. Besides, as soon as she was diagnosed, she wanted to be back home. She stayed with me for a while when she got out of the hospital. Then she decided to go to her parents' farm south of the city, near Priddis. We used to have great parties down there in the old days. I drove her home. It was weird to drive out there again, past the stands of trembling aspen where we'd smoked dope, had uncomfortable but memorable trysts with lovers. I felt guilty.

One day, after one of her surgeries, I went to see her. She was asleep when I arrived. Ian sat with her. For a minute I thought he was asleep, too, the way his chin rested on his chest, but he stood up when I came in.

"Let's go downstairs and have a coffee," he said. "I'm tired of sitting in this room."

In the cafeteria, I noticed Ian had lost weight, so he and Charlotte looked much more alike. When we'd first met, I couldn't believe they were siblings. Ian was on the football team, built like a bull, had dark, wavy hair. Charlotte was willowy, had lighter, straight hair. As far as I knew, the only exercise she ever engaged in was smoking. But now I could see the same sharp planes of cheekbone and jaw in their faces, the same long neck and wide-set eyes. He hadn't shaved in a while, ran his hand over the stubble.

"It's strange, but there's actually been some good about this," he said.

"What could be good about it?"

"I don't mean really good, I mean like consolation prize kind of good. Like at least Charlotte's talking to me again."

"I didn't know she hadn't been."

"Well. I should qualify that. We've talked the last couple of years, but never about anything important. Never anything close to the bone, you know? I'd ask her how she was and she'd say, 'Good,' and then we'd talk about movies or music or stuff in the news, never anything personal. But now we're starting to. I guess being sick like this makes you think about big picture stuff."

"I'm glad. But why weren't you talking about important stuff?"

"For a while, she didn't talk to me at all. She called me up one morning a couple of years ago and asked me to come get her at a bus stop by the university. I hadn't even known she was here, thought she was in Seattle. She'd gotten a ride up here with some friend and had been up at the U the night before waiting for her man in front of one of the buildings. The next thing she knows it's morning and a security guard is kicking the soles of her feet, telling her to move along. She figured the sad part of the story was that she didn't score.

"So I took her home and gave her shit. She wouldn't have any of it. '*You* go to fucking rehab,' she kept saying. Finally, I said the only way she'd ever really get better would be to start accepting herself for what she was. Then she lost it. 'You don't know anything about who I am! Where do you get off telling me how to live?' She stormed out. Even though I didn't even go anywhere near what I was thinking about, I guess I said too much. I thought it might help her. I didn't want to fuck her up."

"I'm sure she knew that deep down. Maybe just not right away."

I said that just to make Ian feel better. I didn't tell him Charlotte had come directly over to my place after this incident.

"My brother's an asshole!" she raged when I opened the door, oblivious to the rain running down her face, soaking her clothes. I hadn't seen her in years and that's what she had to say. I was on my way to work. I made her some tea and told her we'd talk when I got home. She'd crashed on the couch before I even got my shoes on, and when I got back from work she was already gone. That was the last time I saw her before she got sick.

∽

Close to the Bone

When Charlotte and I were both seventeen she lived in an old house downtown with an ever-changing complement of roommates. One hot night when none of the roommates were home, we drank too much red wine, way too fast, in the living room on the brown '50s' couch with the burn holes in the arms. I don't remember now who made the first move, but it didn't matter, the other responded. We got into some passionate necking. Before long we heard someone come into the kitchen through the back door. We managed to get back into presentable positions before John came into the living room.

"Hey, John," said Charlotte casually.

"Hey, ladies. Just having a hen night on the couch, here, are you? Mind if I join you?"

The next evening I called her. "I wanted to talk to you about last night," I said.

"I'm sorry. I'm so sorry. I don't know what happened. I must have been drunk out of my mind."

"Well, we were both drunk, Charlotte. I'm sorry, too."

"I feel terrible about it."

"Listen, it's okay."

"No one can ever know about this, Miriam. No one."

"I won't tell anyone."

Time mellowed me out about that whole incident. Right after it happened I remember being mortified. I felt guilty, awful. For years, every time I thought about it, I felt a sharp twist in my guts, convinced that it would stay on my permanent file. But in the last few years, I look back on it with amusement more than anything. Who cares?

Charlotte, though, I don't know. We couldn't go there. Talking to Ian reminded me that it had been a long time since she and I had talked about anything in any depth, like relationships. Though she'd always had someone. As far as I know she never lived alone. She was afraid to. She'd never been with the same man for any length of time, but I stayed with Mike and got married. I couldn't imagine living the way she did.

∽

I have no memory of getting into bed. Near noon I woke from a dreamless sleep, amazed the phone hadn't rung. I showered, had a sandwich. I thought about calling the hospital before I left but decided not to. What difference would calling make, since I'd be going right up there? Only on the way, I remembered a book on hold for me at the library, and swung by to pick it up. Then I had to get gas. I stood at the pump and looked up at the blue sky, felt the warmth of the sun on my skin. It was all I could do to make myself get back in the car. I tried not to think about spending such a beautiful day in the smell of blood, under the fluorescent lights that made the healthiest flesh look like it came from a jar in a lab, never mind the flesh of the dying.

She was gone when I got there. The door to her room was closed, the morphine pump stood outside. I knew I was too late. Then everything seemed to be underwater for a while. I asked the nurses at the station something, I don't know what. They glubbed something at me I didn't understand. One of them took me into room 763 again. Charlotte looked the same as she had all week, only now she was quiet. A pastoral care worker sat beside Ian, who rested his chin on his chest. We said the Lord's Prayer together.

As we left the hospital, I felt almost giddy with relief for her. It was over, it was over. I drove Ian home and we had a beer, talked for a few hours.

One day about a month later, I went for a walk near the reservoir, felt the wind lift my hair from my shoulders. It occurred to me that Charlotte was dead. We'd gone through all that and nobody had actually said it. They said she'd gone, she'd passed away. But it hit me just then that she was dead. She would not call, she would not drop by. She was dead.

It was a long time before I noticed the warmth of the sun on my skin again.

VALEDICTION

ELIZABETH WATCHED STUDENTS PLAY FRISBEE ON THE frosty grass outside her office window and listened to the message again. It was Lucy Moore, John's sister. She hadn't talked to Lucy in twenty-five years. What could she want? It had to be something about John, probably nothing good.

The morning just seemed to be going that way. First, she'd had an argument with Sally about dropping French.

"Mom, I'll never use it. Why do I have to keep taking something I'm only going to forget anyway?"

How much did that sound like things she'd said herself at that age? "Sally, that's not the point. You want to get into a good university, don't you?"

"I don't even know if I want to go to university. You act like that's a given."

She turned to Mike for support, but he only muttered about an early appointment and left Elizabeth to deal with it. Why did Sally always hit her with this stuff before she'd even had her coffee? And she still smarted from yesterday's department meeting. Wagner implied she'd taught the seventeenth century

Valediction

course for too long, had too much emphasis on Donne. And the department head actually said he'd look into it. Christ.

And now this. Of course maybe Lucy just wanted to catch up. Yeah, right. In any case, she knew she'd never get any meaningful work done until she found out. She called the number.

"Lucy, this is Elizabeth Orlovsky."

"Elizabeth. Thanks for calling back."

"Everything all right?"

"I'm afraid not. John is very ill."

"Oh, no."

"Cancer. It's all over him. They tell us he doesn't have very long, maybe a couple more weeks."

Elizabeth took a deep breath. "Dear God."

"He's at the Baker Centre. I'm sorry to hit you with this out of the blue, but I thought you'd want to know. I know you haven't been in touch with him for a long time, but you two used to be so close. If you want to see him again, you should come as soon as you can."

"I'll try to make it. This is a very busy time for me." *What am I saying?* "I'll let you know."

Some time after she put down the phone, the department admin assistant appeared at her door.

"Dr. Orlovsky? I've been calling you."

"I'm sorry, Carol. I've just had some bad news."

"Oh, I'm sorry. A student is here with an appointment. Should I ask him to reschedule?"

"I'd appreciate that. And I'll be out of my office for the rest of the morning."

"Sure. Anything else I can do?"

"Not right now. Thanks."

She meant to walk along the riverbank, clear her head. But she only made it to a bench outside the library where she sat and stared.

∽

The summer after high school Elizabeth worked as a barmaid at The Calgarian Hotel. That mortified her mother even more than her singing in Life-Size Doll did. The band was fun, but Elizabeth knew she couldn't pay her university tuition with the beer they often got paid in. Anyway, she made good tips as a barmaid. But she'd never been tipped with a book before. The tall, spare fellow with the striking grey eyes and spiky hair paid for his rye and seven, and slipped a tattered paperback onto her tray: *After Many a Summer Dies the Swan* by Aldous Huxley.

She laughed. "What's this?"

"I saw you in the back last week reading *Point Counter Point*. Thought you might be interested."

"Thanks. I'd love to read it. Haven't I seen you before?"

"I saw your band at the hall gig at Hillhurst-Sunnyside a couple of weeks ago."

In the evenings the billiards players and career drinkers sat in the front of The Calgarian, and the punk rockers crowded around the tiny stage in back. One of the old rummies from the pool table side stood unsteadily, waved his arms. "Hey, Blondie," he rasped. "How about some service over here?"

"Hang on," she told him, and turned back to her new friend. "Listen, what's your name?"

"John. You're Liz, right? Liz Lovely."

Valediction

Her face felt hot. That stage name still sounded stupid to her, but it seemed to stick. "Yeah, that's me. I get off in fifteen minutes. Will you still be here?"

"Sure. Can I buy you a drink?"

"I'd love one."

⁓

On the way out of the lecture hall that afternoon, Elizabeth shook her head, amazed at what the mind is capable of while on auto-pilot. Like when she'd arrive somewhere and realize she'd been unaware of driving. Or long ago when she read Sally bedtime stories, fully engaged with the story while thinking of essays she was marking, or a paper she was working on. As she glanced over today's notes on the poetry of Richard Crashaw, she had no memory of discussing his work in class. She couldn't possibly have spent the last fifty minutes fretting out loud, telling the class how angry she was with John. Why hadn't he been the one to call? Why hadn't he called her long ago? Why hadn't he taken better care of himself?

A few years ago she'd heard that John was in a bad way, using again and busking for change outside liquor stores. She hated to think that, though it hadn't surprised her. Lately she'd heard he was better, had been playing jams. And now this. He was only forty-eight.

There was also the problem of going back to Calgary to see him. She wasn't sure how Mike would react.

⁓

It hadn't taken long for Elizabeth to fall in love with John, in spite of a mutual friend's warnings that he'd never gone out with one girl for any length of time. Did she think she was different, did she think she'd be the one to change him? Why hadn't she listened to that well-meaning friend? She wasn't stupid. Though intelligence had nothing to do with it; the first time she caught herself mesmerized by the gold flecks in his irises, it was too late.

At first she loved John's fearlessness, his recklessness. He refused to be held by society's idea of how he should live his life — there was something very romantic about that notion. She had always supposed that he'd eventually grown up, settled down to some degree, but it didn't sound like he had. Until recently, he still did all the same things he'd always done — still played guitar, still did drugs, still drifted from woman to woman. The permanent teenager, never changing. Except for now, maybe.

∾

Elizabeth got ready for bed at her usual time that night, but Mike decided to stay up and watch a movie. Always the movie hound. Of course, the first thing he'd ever said to Elizabeth was, "Here's looking at you, kid," after buying her a drink.

"What is this?" she asked.

"*Anthony Adverse.* 1936, Fredric March and Olivia de Havilland."

"Fredric March looks ridiculous in those pants."

"It's not really his kind of part."

"What, they couldn't get Errol Flynn?"

"Maybe he was busy."

"Maybe. Listen, I need to talk to you about this trip again."

Valediction

He turned and looked at her, stroked his beard. "You want to go to Calgary for a few days because this guy John is dying? This guy you haven't seen in thirty years?"

Elizabeth bristled at the incredulity in his voice, but tried to hold back, tried not to let this become an argument. It would be so easy to yell, so easy to point out that she'd never objected to his stupid overnight hikes with his pot-smoking middle-aged friends, and that this was important. But she wouldn't do that. Yet.

"I have to see him one more time."

"I didn't know you were in touch with him."

"I'm not. His sister called me. Mike, I have to go. All right?"

He turned back to the TV. "Go ahead," he said. She waited for a minute to see if he had anything else to say and then went upstairs.

Oh, Christ. That went over well. Next on the agenda: trying to sleep.

∽

After John's band Dramatis Personae finished a week-long gig at The Calgarian, there'd been a party at the decrepit house on Memorial Drive that some of the band members and hangers-on rented. She and John slunk off to his upstairs bedroom before long, made love for hours to the music that pounded up through the floor. Eventually the music died down and faint light glowed through the holes in the yellow blind. John lit two cigarettes.

"It's already tomorrow," Elizabeth said.

"The good morrow. The day you should quit your job. A girl like you shouldn't work at The Calgarian."

"Why not?"

"It's a hole. What if something happens to you?"

"Nothing will happen. Anyway, my friends all hang out there, they watch out for me. And I make great tips. You have to capitalize on this stuff while you can. Youth and beauty are fleeting."

"So's love," John said.

Elizabeth turned to him, saw her face flicker in his eye for a moment. "It doesn't have to be," she said.

"You're too farsighted. I can't see past the next gig, can't even imagine my life in a year. But you think of stuff fifty years in the future."

"Just making plans, that's all," she answered. He said nothing and soon she heard the regular breath of sleep. She wanted to hold him in her arms like that always, but knew it wouldn't be that way. Maybe for a while, maybe on and off — never always. Sooner or later she would have to stop pretending it was all right, stop pretending she didn't mind. It wasn't all right and she did mind.

As she tried to sleep on the couch downstairs she realized the hardest part was feeling captivated by him and knowing he didn't feel the same way. That was the hardest part by far.

༄

She called Lucy back a couple of days later, almost afraid to. What if he'd died since they'd last talked? While the phone rang, she thought: *please let him hold on*. Finally, Lucy picked up.

"Hi, Elizabeth. I just got back from the hospital."

"How is he?"

Valediction

"Today was a little better than the last few days. He sat up and talked. It was good to see."

Elizabeth's jaw set with fear, apprehension. How bad was he if sitting and talking were big things? "That's good. I'll be there Friday evening."

"Will you stay with your parents?"

"No. They moved to Vancouver Island long ago, and my mom passed away a few years back. I'll be at a hotel on Sixteenth Avenue. Can I call you when I get into town?"

"Sure. I'll probably be visiting him, anyway — do you just want his room number?"

"I don't know. After all this time, I don't know if I can just come up cold, by myself. I know that sounds stupid."

"It's okay. I'll give you my cell number, we'll meet in the lobby. I'll tell John you're coming. It'll give him something to look forward to."

∾

The trouble with teaching English literature, Elizabeth thought as the plane landed, is that bits of poems forever run through your head. She'd had all kinds of death-related ones stuck in there the last few days. In the last few minutes she'd had: *"The breath goes now, and some say, no,"*; *"Death, be not proud / Though some have called thee mighty and dreadful, for thou art not so"*; *"Because I could not stop for Death / He kindly stopped for me."* Christ.

The woman beside her said something. She'd wanted to talk the entire flight, but Elizabeth had kept her nose jammed in a book, though she couldn't really read right then, even after the attendant had brought her scotch. Normally she didn't drink on flights. But this time she felt like a drink. She deserved one. She needed one. She didn't need chit-chat.

"Sorry, what did you say?" asked Elizabeth.

"It's snowing."

"Oh, it is."

It was only the first week of October. But in Calgary there was no such thing as unseasonable snow, or snow too early. She'd seen snow in all months of the year here, and she'd seen temperatures in the twenties in all months of the year, too. You never knew what would blow in over the Rockies.

The snow still fell as she checked into her hotel room. She sat on the blue armchair across from the balcony that faced the river and called Lucy, but got no answer at home or on her cell. She left a message, sat back, watched the snow fall. It reminded her of one of the last times she'd seen John, twenty-five years earlier.

She'd finished with the band by then and had started university. She and John and others of the Dramatis Personae still lived in the house on Memorial Drive. They lived together, yet as John insisted, they didn't "live together" — they were roommates. Their sexual relationship was still exclusive as far as Elizabeth knew. She resented his refusal to commit, he resented her wish for exclusivity. But they couldn't stay away from each other.

She was up late at work on a paper — on Christopher Marlowe or something, that detail had faded. Nobody else was around, John had gone out to see a band. She sat at the kitchen table and listened to a record of Chopin waltzes and mazurkas. She'd come to a lull in the writing process, stared at the falling snow when John came in.

Valediction

"Hey, John," she called. She heard him lock the door, take his boots off.

"Hey, Liz. You still up?"

"Yes."

She got up, saw the tall, black-haired girl in a leather jacket. Could not read the expression on John's face. How could it look so blank? Before she could speak they'd started up the stairs.

"Goodnight, Liz," he called.

She went back to the kitchen and lit a cigarette. "Goodbye, John," she whispered. She moved out the next day, left before he woke up. The girl was gone. He slept undisturbed while she took her things out of the bedroom.

Over the next weeks she came back to the house a few times to pick up things. He was always there when she came, sullen and quiet, drinking. The very last time she'd seen him she'd said goodbye to him as she left and he hadn't even bothered to answer. That hurt, it hurt for a long time, but she'd dealt with it years ago. Would there be another goodbye?

Why didn't Lucy pick up? Of course, you weren't supposed to even have your phone turned on in hospital rooms, were you? Something about them interfering with the equipment. Maybe she was just out of range.

She decided to call the hospital herself. She got as far as looking up the main number for the Tom Baker Centre but then hesitated. She was afraid, didn't want to have to do this, didn't want to see him as he lay dying. She wanted to remember him the way he was.

Then Lucy called.

"Elizabeth. I'm sorry I couldn't call before," she choked. "I'm sorry — it's too late. He died this afternoon. I tried to call you at home, but I guess you'd already left. I'm sorry."

My hands feel cold, Elizabeth noticed as she rubbed a throbbing spot on her temple with her free hand.

"Elizabeth?" Lucy asked.

"I'm still here. I'm the one who should be sorry. I should have left as soon as you called that morning."

"He tried to hold on. He wanted to see you. But it was just too much at the end."

Lucy sounded so tired, Elizabeth thought after she got off the phone. She remembered when her mother died of cancer. The late nights, the stress. The horror. It takes a toll on everybody.

Never send to know for whom the bell tolls; it tolls for thee.

Elizabeth left the hotel to find an open liquor store. She thought about having a drink in the hotel lounge but she might start to cry, and she wouldn't do that in front of a room full of strangers. She'd bring something back to her room and have a drink while she called Mike.

∽

"Are you staying for the funeral?" Mike asked.

"I suppose I should since I'm here. They'll probably have it fairly soon. In the meantime I'll try to get in touch with Charlotte, maybe a couple of other old friends."

"Well, take your time. You don't need to rush back. We're fine."

That was good, she thought when she hung up. She could take her time. But then maybe he meant he didn't care *when*

Valediction

she came back. She sighed, found the Gideon Bible and the phone book in a drawer. She thought about looking up the 23rd Psalm but decided instead to look up Charlotte's number in the phone book. There was no reply.

She picked up the Bible again and flipped, not to the 23rd Psalm, but to The Song of Solomon.

"Let him kiss me," she read aloud, "With the kisses of his mouth: for thy love is better than wine."

She poured another glass of wine, put the book away. John's mouth, she remembered, always tasted of cigarettes. Hers must have, too. She thought of their tongues locked, tasting of cigarettes and Calgarian Hotel draft. She remembered other things about him that she thought she'd forgotten: the scar on his forehead above his right eye from a fight, the small gold hoop in his left ear (did he still wear it?), the feel of his lean, wiry body against hers, warm arms wrapped around her. She'd wanted to feel him up against her, feel his arms encircle her one last time.

She hadn't been going to think about this, until now had made an effort to avoid thinking about it. But she allowed her mind to wander back to a night when she and John had lain in bed with a battered copy of *Palgrave's Golden Treasury*, one of the first poetry anthologies Elizabeth had ever owned, picked up at the long-gone old Hillhurst Book Store for a dime. They took turns reading to each other, poems by Shakespeare, Yeats, Matthew Arnold, Walt Whitman, Thomas Hardy. And John Donne. John's voice was raspy by the time he read, *Sweetest love, I do not go / For weariness of thee . . .* She'd watched his gold-flecked eyes move over the lines on the page and then move over her face.

It was past one AM. Elizabeth sat alone on a Thursday night in a Calgary hotel room, drunk, watching the snow fall. John was dead. *I didn't even get a chance to say goodbye*, she thought. *I didn't even get a chance to tell him — to tell him how pissed off at him I am, angry at him like I haven't been in years. Because he brought all this stuff up again. I was living my life, I was doing fine and then he has to go and stir up all this shit again. Typical of him. Some things never change.*

If only that were really true.

∽

The funeral was the next Wednesday, a cool, bright morning. Mass was held at the family's Catholic church. A closed casket service, Elizabeth was relieved to see. Perhaps it was selfish, but she wanted to remember him the way he was. It was good to see Lucy again. She looked much the same, though tired, so tired, not surprisingly.

There were a few of the old punk crowd in attendance, though not as many as she would have thought. At the reception afterwards, over and over, she heard amazement from many of them that John had lived as long as he had. She had always supposed that he'd eventually grown up, settled down to some degree, but it sounded like he'd lived recklessly all along. It didn't really make his end less sad, or less tragic, but somehow it made Elizabeth feel a little better about how things had ended up between them. Their end had been inevitable. And she had moved on, even if she'd been briefly brought back to those days.

∽

Valediction

Mike rushed up to her in the airport and Elizabeth realized they hadn't embraced that way in a long time. It felt good to have his arms around her, to smell his faint scent of coffee and soap.

"How's Sally?" she asked as they pulled out of the parkade.

"*Tres bien, madame.* She'll stick with French for now. She was actually surprisingly reasonable when we talked about it. Maybe she missed you or something. Though I did overhear her talking to a friend on the phone, saying we *made* her keep taking it."

"Well, she's got to save face with her friends. You know how that goes. But I'm relieved you managed to change her mind. And listen, thanks for coming to get me. You didn't have to."

"It's all right. I thought the last few days might have been a little rough. I'm sorry about the way I acted before you left. I know John meant a lot to you once."

"That's okay. It was a surprise."

"It's too bad you didn't get to see him. But maybe in a way it's better like this."

"I think so. I came to terms with what happened between us long ago, back when you think a broken heart is the worst thing that can happen to you. Better to remember him the way he was."

"Besides," Mike said. "You'll always have Paris."

Elizabeth shook her head. It was impossible to say what was worse, the corny movie quote or the fact that she knew what he meant. But she laughed anyway.

Fiction Romance

I'D BEEN LOVE WITH NEIL FOR AGES. But he had no idea, and whenever I was around him, I'd be struck dumb with shyness. Worse, he'd gone to spend the summer with relatives on the West Coast. The whole thing depressed me. My best friend Alice also happened to be in the unrequited love field. Naturally, we talked about our troubles, my love for Neil and hers for Matt. We talked about them a good deal; some would say too much. Perhaps we did, at that.

We'd call each other at night and talk for hours. "Ever wonder what it would be like, Leah," she asked me once, "if Neil were driving down the street, and saw you, and slowed down?"

That particular scenario hadn't entered my mind, I told her, and stretched out on my bed.

"No? Well, what if it was a rainy night during World War II and you were on your way home from your swing shift at a munitions plant, in a threadbare coat, getting soaked to the skin, walking home because you were broke? And Neil was driving — no, wait, being chauffeured in a limousine. He's a general, and he sees this poor woman getting soaked, and tells the driver to pull over and offer her a ride home. Normally, you wouldn't accept, but you're so wet and tired and cold that you decide to take a chance. You sit down beside him, give the driver your address as the limo pulls away. You turn to thank him, and realize it's Neil. You haven't seen each other in years. He looks fantastic, very suave in his uniform. The grey sets off his green eyes and blond hair. You feel embarrassed sitting beside him in your faded dress and old coat, but he's delighted to see you, and the two of you chat like the years haven't slid by at all. Until the driver pulls up outside your scroddy apartment building." She paused. "Should I go on?"

I swallowed. "Sure."

"He tells you it's been wonderful to see you again, and you realize he's holding your frozen hand in his warm one. You invite him in for a drink, almost afraid to watch his face for the reaction. He says he'd love to, and sends the driver home.

"You tell him to make himself at home, find the bottle of brandy you've been saving for a special occasion, and pour two glasses. He sits close to you on the couch, closer after some brandy.

"'Your stockings,' he tells you, 'are spattered with mud. I hope my driver didn't do that. Here, let me help you take them off.'

"You reach under your skirt and undo the garters. Gently, slowly he rolls the left stocking down your leg, slides it off your foot, then rolls the other stocking off. He caresses your feet, kisses them in turn.

"'These poor little feet. Such beautiful feet should not have to be stood on hour after hour, day after day. They should be bathed in rosewater, pedicured, massaged every day.'

"Then his hands run slowly, purposefully, up your shins, over your knees, to your trembling thighs — "

"Hang on a second, Alice. I have to get my cigarettes."

After she finished her tale, I was inspired to reciprocate with one of my own featuring Alice as a demure but irrepressibly sensuous model and Matt as a staid but secretly passionate and extremely long-winded painter. It was past 1:00 AM when we finally got off the phone. I laid my head on my pillow, faint smell of a rain-soaked, grey wool uniform in my nostrils, and slept.

∽

And so it went. We made no mention of the stories when we saw each other in person. But during another phone call a few days later, we found ourselves swapping erotic tales again. Before long, we were at it every night. Soon we just dispensed with the small talk almost immediately and got right to the stories. They got better, more daring. We started to fill in the details in places where we once said 'and the cloud went over the moon'.

I don't know about Alice, but I know I spent quite a few daytime hours dreaming up ideas for our nighttime phone calls. I'd taken some extra hours at Eaton's doing inventory. It wasn't just that I needed the money, I also thought if I kept busy it would help me get my mind off things. How wrong I was. Counting towels and shower-curtain rings and cutlery alone in a hot stockroom was definitely not the way to stop thinking about Neil; it was the way to think about nothing else all day. Even on my breaks in the cafeteria, my mind wandered away from the novels I tried to read.

In the meantime, Alice and I were definitely onto something. But was it a good thing or a bad thing? I was pretty sure it was a weird thing. Thinking about the ramifications too much made me uncomfortable. I didn't tell anybody about it and I don't think she did, either. A couple of times, we blushed when we saw each other in the hard light of day. Sometimes I felt guilty about it, vowed more than once to stop. But I was lonely. And it was so easy. Besides, I didn't want Alice to think I was a prude. Just once more can't hurt, anyway, I kept telling myself.

∾

Alice went away with her parents for a long weekend. I didn't think it would bother me. She'd only be gone three nights. The first night I went to a movie. I was fine, I was fine, I hardly even thought about talking to Alice. The second night was a little harder. First, I started to read, but I couldn't keep my mind on the book. I ended up plotting out my stories for Monday night, when Alice would be back, even made some notes. I also got a few ideas in reserve for future nights.

The third night was rough. The day had been too hot to do much of anything but stay out of the sun. When it finally cooled off a bit in the evening, I went for a walk. To clear my mind was the idea, but it didn't actually help much. I started to wonder, as I stopped for smokes and a pop, if Alice was as disturbed about missing our phone calls as I was. She probably wasn't. She probably didn't even care. Here I was, miserable and distracted, while she was off enjoying herself, not even thinking about me at all. It wasn't fair. By the time I got home I was furious. I got some magazines from the house and sat out on the patio, flipping through them, determined not to think about Alice and her selfishness. I heard the phone ring and started to get up to answer it. Then I decided not to. She was the one who went away, she was the one making me suffer. Let her think I was out having a good time, a far better time than I'd be having talking to her all night. The phone stopped ringing. In a few minutes, it rang again, and still I would not answer. When it stopped, I felt a bizarre little twinge of victory.

Alice returned the next day and called at the usual time, said she'd missed our calls. I was cool, indifferent, didn't let on what I'd felt over the weekend. But we talked late into the night.

~

Near the end of the summer, I ran into Neil's older sister, Sandra, downtown. She looked just like Neil, only she had long hair. I always found talking to her a little jarring. I forced myself to wait a polite amount of time until I asked about Neil.

"Neil? Oh, he's fine. I just talked to him last night."

"So I guess he'll be home pretty soon," I suggested, trying not to sound too interested.

"No, actually. That was why he called. He's got a job in Victoria. At first it was just supposed to be for the summer, but they asked him if he'd want to stay on permanently and he finally made up his mind and said yes. He wants me to send some of his stuff out on the Greyhound."

"Really?"

"Yeah, isn't that great? You know, he told me he's been trying to call you, for weeks, but when he gets off work at ten-thirty, your phone is always busy. For hours, he said. He wanted to know if I'd heard anything about you having a boyfriend, and I said I hadn't. But it looks to me like you're not getting much sleep these days. You've got dark circles under your eyes. C'mon, who is he?"

Oh, Lord, not the elbow in the side. I might throw up. "Nobody. I'm just a little under the weather."

The smirk on her face made it plain that she didn't believe me. "Well, you ought try to get a good night's sleep tonight. Do you wonders. Listen, I've got to run, but it was good to see you."

"You, too. And send Neil my, uh, regards, would you?"

∽

When Alice called that night I told her the whole sordid story.

"Well, Leah. I'm very sorry to hear all of that. I don't really know what to say."

"There's not much *to* say. I guess this will just go on record as the worst summer of my life, that's all."

"Listen, what if you were to get a job on The Queen of Esquimalt?"

"On the what?"

"You know, one of those ferries. Maybe you could work in the kitchen or something. And maybe one day he'll go to Vancouver and happen to fall overboard, and when they pull him up you can give him mouth-to-mouth."

"I think it's time we put an end to the stories, don't you? I mean, after today, I just don't have the heart for it anymore."

"Yeah. I guess you're right. And anyway, I can't talk very long tonight. I've got a date with Matt."

"You're kidding."

"No. We're going to a movie. Aren't you happy for me?"

"I am. Really, it's great. I've just had kind of a rotten day, that's all."

When I got off the phone with Alice the clock said 8:30. I didn't do much. I didn't feel like going to sleep yet, so I sat and smoked and looked out the window, watched it get dark. I thought for a while about calling Sandra and getting Neil's number from her, for all the good it would do. For one thing, I was sure that I'd stutter like an idiot if I even got up the courage to call him. And how would I explain about my phone being busy every night, all summer? Besides, he'd taken that job. There was no point. I turned on the light eventually and tried to read a little bit. But I couldn't concentrate. The silence of the phone not ringing echoed hollowly in the back of my throat. Finally, I went to bed at eleven-thirty.

The phone didn't ring once.

Acknowledgements

My thanks to Rona Altrows and Diane Girard for their thoughtful reading, unfailing encouragement and invaluable friendship through the writing of these stories. Love and thanks always to Bruce, Nick and Dan for keeping me anchored in reality. I am grateful to the editors of the following publications, where some of these stories have appeared previously:

"Leading Men" in *Prairie Fire*

"Art is Long" in *The Fiddlehead*

"Nothing Sacred" in *FreeFall* and *Red Light: Superheroes, Saints and Sluts* (anthology) (Arsenal Pulp Press, 2005)

"Blue Lake" in *The Antigonish Review*

"We Had Faces Then" in *The Wingham Advance-Times*

"Rain in December" in *The Amethyst Review*

"The Pass" in *Alberta Anthology 2005* (Red Deer Press, 2005)

An earlier version of "The Least She Could Do" in *FreeFall*

"The Selfish Professor" in *The Prairie Journal*

"Across the Universe" and "Hamburg Blues" in *Transition*

"You Tore Me Down" in *C / Oasis*

"Sisters of Mercy" in *Forum* (Calgary Women's Writing Project)

"Bells and Whistles" in *Spoiled Ink*

"Beware of God" in *The Plum Ruby Review*

"Close to the Bone" in *Room*

"Fiction Romance" in *The Nashwaak Review*

Author photo by Jennifer Tzanakos

LORI HAHNEL recently leaped onto the Canadian fiction scene with her fall 2008 novel *Love Minus Zero* (Oberon Press). *Nothing Sacred* is her second publication, which features her award-winning short fiction that has been broadcast on CBC Radio, and widely published in anthologies and journals including *The Fiddlehead*, *Room Magazine*, and *Prairie Fire*. A three-time Journey Prize nominee, she has been shortlisted in the *Prism International* Short Fiction contest and nominated for National and Western Magazine Awards. Born in Regina, Saskatchewan, her family moved to Calgary, Alberta in 1974, where she currently resides with her husband and sons.

Author's website: www.lorihahnel.ca

ENVIRONMENTAL BENEFITS STATEMENT

Thistledown Press saved the following resources by printing the pages of this book on chlorine free paper made with 100% post-consumer waste.

TREES	WATER	SOLID WASTE	GREENHOUSE GASES
7 FULLY GROWN	3,317 GALLONS	201 POUNDS	689 POUNDS

Calculations based on research by Environmental Defense and the Paper Task Force.
Manufactured at Friesens Corporation